Prince of the Mist

by Penelope Marzec

For Tommy, My Irish Grandfather
A True Leprechaun

Chapter One

Tia suppressed the moan in her throat. Clutching the ache on her right side, she turned to continue running. She glanced around the level plateau but saw only the tall trees and the shadowing canopy of the forest where the light faded as the sun set over the tops of the Catskill Mountains. She needed someplace to hide but there were no large rocks. The trees, while tall, were not wide and would offer precious little camouflage. With a sickening sense of despair, she knew she couldn't go much further since the searing pain in her side would not allow her to take a decent breath.

She staggered along the leaf-strewn ground until a stabbing pain in her shoulder halted her in her tracks for a moment. She tried to catch her breath, but breathing caused a spasm of agony in her side. She hit the ground hard when she escaped from the carjacker and now she could not bear to move her shoulder even the slightest bit or fill her lungs with air.

So far there had been no gunshots, but her pursuer had a weapon and at any rate he would overpower her when he caught her. She leaned against the rough bark of a tree and closed her eyes for a moment, swallowing against the tightness in her throat. She did not want to die, but she could not fight off the madman.

When she opened her eyes again, a sudden wind stirred through the branches overhead as a thick fog began to roll toward her like a shroud, obliterating the landscape with a blanket of mist. The bizarre haze spread quickly, deadening the noise in the woods and making it eerily quiet--save for a muffled shout from the carjacker.

She tried to move away from the icy white dampness but it followed her, swirling around faster and faster, as though it wanted to envelop her. Already numb with fear, she found her terror spiraling out of control with the cold cloud smothering her.

A large fallen log lay a couple feet away. She was sure it

had not been there a few moments before, but she headed toward it nevertheless, gritting her teeth as every movement of her side shot an excruciating ache through her.

Suddenly, there in the dancing fog, she spotted a backpacker standing on the other side of the log. The tall blond man had such fair skin that even in the dying light, his face was plainly visible. He beckoned to her. For a moment, she hesitated. What if he was a friend of the carjacker?

"This way," he called.

Something in his voice reassured her. Glancing behind, she saw nothing save for the white fog. Her heart thundered as she staggered toward the log. It was far more massive than she had thought at first, level with the middle of her thigh.

"Swing your legs over," the backpacker urged.

Another shout echoed through the forest from the maniac pursuing her. That spurred her on as terror flooded through her veins. The searing pain from her side threatened to immobilize her, but she managed to swing her right leg over the trunk, then her left.

The backpacker gave her a warm smile and held out his hand. She reached for it and at the first touch, she found an odd sensation flooding through her--a weightlessness that made her lightheaded.

"Jump!" the backpacker implored.

Looking beneath her, Tia saw only the leaf-covered floor of the forest. She pushed off the rough bark and found herself sliding right through the leaves and down into empty darkness.

She screamed in panic. She could see nothing as she fell further and further. Was it a rabbit hole? A bear den? Tia felt the backpacker's hand still clutching hers, but she could hear nothing except the howl of the wind. Twisting through the empty space, she saw her whole life pass before her in a brief instant. Somewhere, far off, she thought she heard lilting music. Then all sounds, even the sound of rushing air stopped as she passed out cold.

* * * *

At first, Tia could not open her eyes, but she did not care. Light hands soothed her--like feathery breaths of wind against her skin. Her shoulder and side no longer ached. She floated serenely in her fantasy world while soft, lilting music played somewhere above her. She dreamed she was the bride in a beautiful wedding and when she took the hand of a handsome groom, he smiled at her with such radiance that warmth flowed all the way through her, chasing away the chill of her evening in the forest.

Then she rested peacefully, thinking of nothing, her mind emptied of fear or want until one hand pressed heavily upon her shoulder. An intense heat spread from that touch and started the return of the memories. She did not want them for they were too painful, but she could not stop the flood of information from pouring back. All the peace and tranquility left her. The nightmare of the carjacking ... the carjacker leering at her ... her desperate escape ... the sense of hopelessness ... the odd fog in the forest ... the backpacker holding out his hand. Had she survived or was she in heaven?

Cautiously, she opened her eyes. Light poured down on her from above, illumination so blinding that she had to turn her head to the side. Squinting against the brightness, she saw him. His hand lay on her shoulder while he sat next to the bed on which she lay. The eyes gazing back at her were a soft, light green. For a moment, Tia was mesmerized by the color. He gave her an appealing smile, which she found open and friendly. Tentatively, she smiled back. This was the handsome groom she had dreamed about and the backpacker who had taken her hand in the forest. Was he an angel?

As he leaned forward, she realized that the chair he sat in looked as if it had been carved from jade. Solid jade, the precious and expensive gemstone. The color of his eyes matched the hue of the chair.

"Do you think you're ready for a sip of clover nectar?" He held out a jewel-encrusted golden chalice.

"So ... this is heaven." It wasn't exactly what she had expected but nobody really knew what waited in the world beyond.

His deep chuckle disturbed her. "No, this is the Sifra, or at least a small part of it."

She noticed that his smile had a sensuous tilt to it, which did something phenomenal to her heart rate.

"Who are you?"

"I'm Wildon, Sidhe chief of the Catskill environment." He slid his hand away from her and leaned back in the chair. She felt chilled without his touch.

On his head, he wore a ring of gold that glinted in the glowing rays shining down on them. He sighed and removed the circlet, setting it on a small table that appeared to be made of carved ivory.

Tia rubbed her eyes. He did not have wings. If this wasn't heaven, then the chair and the table must be made of plastic, the chalice and crown of brass.

"You don't look like a Native American."

"The Sidhe have been here longer than the Native American tribes, and actually there are more of us."

She hesitated. She knew American history very well.

"I'm not surprised that you know nothing of the Sidhe. Most humans dismiss the entire race as nothing more than a bedtime story." He sighed.

Warning bells went off in Tia's head. She furrowed her brow and studied Wildon suspiciously. Lifting a hand to her temple, she decided it might be better to play dumb. She mumbled. "I must have hit my head--or something--when I fell."

"You've been restored to complete health."

"Oh." She prodded her side, searching for the ache that had caused such excruciating pain, but she didn't even feel a tenderness there. "Is this a hospital?"

His eyes darkened a shade. "As some humans would say, this is where I crash."

Mixed feelings swirled through her. "You were the backpacker. I reached for your hand. Aren't you a doctor, too, or a nurse, or something?"

"No. As I said, I'm a Sidhe chief, son of the king. I feared the man chasing you had evil intent so I brought you here."

"Did the police catch him?"

His pointed scrutiny had fear knotting inside her.

"I really do not know."

"But my car ... by the narrow bridge--a silver gray sedan."

He simply shook his head.

She pressed her lips together, willing herself not to break

into tears over the lost car and the carjacker who had gotten away. Resolving to be strong, she sat up and threw back the satin sheets.

She gasped when she saw that she wore a white gown made of an unusual filmy fabric. It clung to her every curve. Flushing in anger, she shot out questions.

"What happened to my clothes? What kind of outfit is this?"

"It's just the uniform of the day--and a wonderful day it has been." He wore a look of satisfaction as he fingered the tunic he wore. It, too, was white and made of some diaphanous material that had gold fibers glittering with every move he made--even with every breath he took.

She couldn't help staring at him, especially the part of him below the short tunic. He had incredible legs, the kind she had only seen in magazines--the kind she believed had been manipulated by a clever graphic artist to look better than actual skin. She could hardly believe that such perfection existed-- especially on a man.

She started to breathe faster. Then she looked up again at his face and saw the flicker of amusement in his gaze. Could he know what she had been thinking? She felt the blush burn on her cheeks.

"I want my own clothes back!" she insisted.

"You must be properly dressed in the Sifra."

Once more he held out the golden goblet. "I know you're terribly thirsty--and this would do you a world of good." He winked at her. "That's another human phrase I picked up. I really enjoy all the idioms--the way your people toy with the language--it has so many nuances. Our language is so stilted and stale. It hasn't changed much at all since Creation."

She did not take the goblet. She glared at him.

"Is this a cult?" She narrowed her eyes and watched while his gaze meandered intimately over her body. She found a curious heat blazing along the trail of his bold stare.

"Perhaps you could say that what we have here is an alternative lifestyle."

There was an intensity to him that sent her pulse throbbing. She didn't know exactly what was going on, but she found her response to this stranger clouded her thinking.

"So you smoke grass and run around in these filmy robes and--and--and--"

"Make love?" He raised his eyebrows with the question.

She barely nodded and she realized that her pulse began to race with speculation. With his broad shoulders, strong neck, and his long, wavy blond hair, he reminded her of a surfer-- minus the tan. She had seen few men in such amazing shape. A flood of wanting surged through her. However, she could not allow herself to be swept away.

"I am leaving. Right now." She stood up and swayed precariously.

He quickly rose and caught her elbow to steady her. "I don't think you're quite ready to go running through the woods yet. What is it they say, 'haste makes waste'?"

Her own mother was very fond of that particular saying. Tia took a deep breath and turned to face him. However, his jade-colored eyes nearly entranced her once more and an odd tingling spread through her. Still, she had to be firm, she reminded herself.

"Look, I appreciate the fact that you saved me from that maniac, but I really must get back."

His smile faded and it seemed as if the light above her dimmed. "There's one important detail--"

"I'm out of here!" She yanked her arm away from him and turned to look for an exit. It only took her a few seconds to realize that the room did not have a door. She ran her hands around the walls in a panic. "Get me out of here. Let me out!" She pounded the wall with her fists as fright tore through her.

When he encased her trembling hands in his, a soothing warmth shimmered up her arms. His gaze turned into a soft caress. It was like gazing at graceful aspen leaves fluttering in the breeze.

"We must wait for the council's decision."

She could feel the hysteria rising in her throat.

"Am I a prisoner? With you?"

"Think of it as a holding pattern."

He said it calmly, as if being in a room with no door did not merit her concern. Simply the tone of his voice composed her to a small degree, but the fact remained that she could not leave. He gave her hands a tender squeeze and she felt a current go through her, one that raced along her veins to her heart. Still, the walls hemmed her in.

"There is no way out. I am trapped." Her voice caught on a sob.

"We shouldn't be here much longer."

In the tense silence that followed his words her body longed for more of his touch, but she refused to allow herself to surrender. How could she trust him? With a quick movement that caught him off guard, she pulled her hands away from his and picked up the golden chalice. Holding it high, she intended to use it as a weapon.

"I don't believe you. You shut me up in here!" Her whole body quaked. "Get me out *now*!"

He eyed the chalice and shrugged. "The taste of clover nectar is as good as it gets, but oh well...." When he snapped his fingers, the heavy chalice became a snake.

Tia screamed in terror and dropped the snake. The animal quickly slithered away and disappeared--gliding through the wall.

"He was harmless, merely a rat snake, but it was a rather large one and black, of course, which made it seem far more sinister than it was." Wildon sat down in the jade chair and placed the circlet of gold back on his head.

Tia backed up against the opposite wall--as far away from Wildon as she could get in the close confines of the cell.

"Tell me you're a magician. Tell me that was only a trick. Tell me I wasn't really seeing and holding a snake." She choked on the last word.

"It was a snake," he admitted in a gentle voice. "The Sidhe are capable of manipulating reality to some extent. I guess you might say it's a genetic tendency."

Her breath came in heaving gasps. She wrapped her arms around herself and took in a deep gulp of air.

"Why don't you manipulate a door into the wall?" She shouted the question, feeling herself on the verge of insanity.

He folded his hands and regarded her with a degree of gravity. In the hush, she could hear her heart thumping. She swallowed past the tightness in her throat. Sitting in the ornate chair with the circlet of gold upon his head, he looked almost regal--more than that, more than some ordinary earthly prince, she decided. He looked like a god. His power wrapped around her, and she realized that it was not the confines of the room that made her nearly breathless, but his nearness.

"It is a matter of honor," he finally stated.

She nodded, uncertain how to proceed under the circumstances.

"Okay. Let's start all over. What is this 'Shee'? Is that like S-H-E-I-K, you know the guys with the turbans?"

"Nope. S-I-D-H-E. In past times, humans called us the Good People. I think it was a more meaningful term. Nowadays, humans have a bad habit of referring to us as fairies."

"F-f-fairies? You mean like--you're gay?" An unsettling wave of disappointment washed through her.

"No."

She detected the frost in his answer.

"I'll lay all my cards on the table--as a human would say." His low tone sounded almost seductive to her. "Humans have many legends about the origin of the Sidhe. Some say they were fallen angels, brought to earth by the sin of pride. Some claimed the Sidhe were gods--that is until the Christians came along and abolished that idea. Yet, the reality is that we are immortal--at least as long as we remain in the Sifra."

A minute before, she would have asked him in a virulently sarcastic manner what he had been smoking. Now, she weighed his words carefully. After all, she had felt the scales on that snake. It lent everything another perspective.

"I thought fairies--or the Sidhe as you call yourself--lived in Ireland, England, and Scotland."

"We are everywhere. The Persians called us the Peris. The Egyptians and the Greeks thought of us as demons--though allies to them. No human can seem to grasp the concept."

He stood up again. He towered over Tia, yet she realized that she did not fear him.

"You don't die? At all?"

"Eventually, on Judgment Day, we get annihilated--or in human terms, fried. But immortality isn't all it's cracked up to be," he mused while drumming his fingers on the small ivory table.

Tia studied his hands. There did seem to be magic in his

touch. She had never believed in any kind of sorcery, and all the New Age stuff she dismissed as nonsense. However, Wildon seemed to possess something inexplicable where her heart was concerned. Fire sparked inside her and a languid heat suffused her core.

"Humans get a better deal and eternal life in the end--the whole enchilada, you might say." A touch of misery shaded his features. "Forever can be a long time without someone to love." He turned his back to her and she heard his deep sigh.

She knew what it was like to be alone, and it was difficult not to sympathize with him. Sure, her plant nursery kept her busy, but there were nights when she sat all by herself in her cabin and wondered why she had a little ache in her heart.

Still, sharing a windowless, doorless cell with the most handsome guy she had ever met didn't engender a feeling of relaxation. She *was* a prisoner.

"If you live here in the Sifra, where did you pick up so much slang?"

He faced her once more. She could see that her question put him into a better frame of mind.

"Lately, the council has been concerned about how the humans are treating the earth--after all, we have to share it. Therefore, the council, on a trial basis, is allowing some of us to try and teach people to respect the environment. I joined the Sierra Club, the Audubon Society, and the Northern Forest Activists Network. I do enjoy your society, but they have a lot to learn, Tia."

She sucked in her breath. "How do you know my name?"

"You had a driver's license on you."

"Oh. Right."

A well of sadness hit her as she thought about her missing car and tears formed in her eyes, but she went on with her false bravado.

"And I insist upon getting that license back immediately!"

"That is beyond my control."

Tia's nerves snapped. "I have to get back to work. My mother will be frantic if I don't give her a call. Please, *please* do something."

His manner became stiff and his eyes seemed shuttered, as if a secret lay hidden there and he did not want her to see it.

"Other humans who have stumbled into the Sifra never want to leave. All the lost treasures of the world belong to the Sidhe."

"I don't care about treasures!" Tia cried. "I want to go home!"

"That is not your decision. You are my bride."

Chapter Two

Wildon had spent much of the past year in human company on a regular basis. He had seen plenty of humans get hot under the collar, especially when it came to environmental issues.

He stepped back when he noticed Tia's face turning as fiery as her brilliant hair. He adored the color of her hair, it reminded him of the sun going down over the mountains. However, as he saw her ball her delicate hands into fists and felt the heat emanating from her body, he recognized all the signs of anger.

"I definitely did not say 'I do' to you. I've been unconscious!"

Wildon flinched at her tone of voice.

"We *are* married," he emphasized. "My father, the king, conducted the ceremony. You are far lovelier to me than any Sidhe I have ever known. You are the woman I have chosen."

He thought he could mollify her by stating the truth in a reasonably quiet manner, but his calm demeanor did not change her stance. She stamped her foot, put her hands on her hips, and glared at him with sapphire fury.

"I did *not* give you my consent and therefore I did *not* marry you."

Wildon sighed. Humans were such sticklers for trivia. He rubbed his palms together and clapped. The marriage certificate appeared and he held it out for her to see.

"That is an obvious fake! You pulled it out of your--your tunic!"

"I don't do card tricks." Wildon crumpled the certificate in his hand and closed his fist tightly around the wadded up paper. Then he opened his hand and showed her that it was empty. He waited for a moment until she realized that a gold ring with the intersecting lines of a Celtic design had appeared on her finger.

"Hey!" She tugged at it in vain.

"You cannot remove it," he told her.

He saw her spin around and start pacing back and forth in the small room.

"My mother is a lawyer. You can't get away with this. She is also a New York state senator and she is going to win the next presidential election. If I don't get home, she is going to tear the mountains down until she finds me!"

A sense of unease gripped Wildon. He recognized the love and admiration in Tia's face. He expected it since Angela Glenmore was her mother. However, while Senator Glenmore did have strong support from her political party, she did not have the backing of any of the environmental groups--and with good reason. She favored nuclear power. Worse, what she thought would be a good location for a new nuclear plant happened to be directly over the Sifra.

Thinking about a meltdown above his home made him feel ill. He struggled to keep his voice courteous. "You do not know who will win the presidency. Some humans favor the current president, though some do not. Many of those in the environmental groups claim to favor the Green Party. Angela Glenmore is clearly not mindful of environmental issues."

"That is ridiculous! My mother is very concerned about the environment--especially since I own a plant nursery and inform her about all the issues."

"Did you hear what she said about the proposed nuclear plant?"

"Um--I'm sure she was misquoted!"

He saw her determination falter as she touched her forehead.

"Maybe I'm just delirious. Maybe this is a nightmare and I'm not really here at all."

A fragile note sounded in her voice. Wildon, like all Sidhe, could not bear unhappiness--light and gaiety reigned perpetually in the palace. Her misery weighed on him. He moved closer to her and touched her shoulder lightly.

"If this was only a dream, I wouldn't be here as well," he said in an attempt to point out the obvious.

"Sure." She sniffed. "You're the best looking hunk I've ever seen. You mean to tell me those pectorals are real?"

Wildon glanced at his chest. "As you humans say, 'The proof is in the pudding.' You can touch me." He lifted her hand

and placed it on his chest.

He heard her small gasp as her skin connected with his. He felt the current flashing between them and knew he had chosen well--despite the fact that she was a human. He closed his eyes and felt the warmth of her skin pulsing through his own. Humans always generated an incredible amount of heat and expended vast quantities of energy, but this one young woman radiated such a shimmering glow that a delightful joy coursed through him with her pulse. It was better than touching the smooth, sun-baked rocks in an icy stream--better than standing in the moonlight on the mountaintop. His other hand slid down to her side so that he could gently pull her closer to him.

"Let me go!"

She startled him by shoving him away. He opened his eyes in bewilderment.

"You--you keep your hands to yourself!"

She let out a great sob and threw herself onto the bed. He knew she was crying, but he didn't know what magic he could use to fix the problem. No one ever cried in the Sifra. He had seen humans cry a few times--and other humans usually handed them a small piece of soft paper--a tissue, they called it. He could make a tissue.

With a wave of his hand, he soon had a soft tissue to hand to her. He gave it to her, and she snatched at it, but that didn't stop her tears. He knelt beside her and stroked her beautiful hair. She wore it short, a small cap of color that framed her sweetly shaped face.

"Don't cry, Tia. It is a great honor to be married to the son of the king. I thought it would please you."

A small drop of water rolled down her cheek. He caught it with his finger and tasted it. It contained the essence of the sea.

"*Please* let me go home. I have to get back to my business."

Hearing her beg had Wildon's eyes clouding, too. He had never known such agony. It felt as if a knife had been thrust into his chest.

He waved his hand and produced another tissue from the air. He dabbed at the dampness on her face.

"Your skin is as smooth as new mushrooms, and your eyes are the color of the mountain lakes--there is not another Sidhe maiden in all the world as beautiful as you."

"M-mushrooms? I'm married to a fairy who looks better than a male model, but he thinks my skin looks like a fungus."

He heard her sniff and then a small bubble of laughter rose from her throat. The sound, though ever so tenuous, cheered him.

"But it does, see the color--so pale, and then when I run my hand along your arm, it is so smooth--just like a mushroom." He touched her, and the warmth of her tender flesh nearly intoxicated him. Shivers rippled through her and he knew that she, too, found pleasure in the contact.

He gazed down into her eyes and recognized the longing in them--a sad and lonely hunger that had lain dormant for years. The intensity of his own feelings jolted him to the core. Never before had he been so entranced and the overwhelming power of his emotions confused him.

He reached out with his finger to trace the edge of her hairline and found a curl that framed her ears in a most charming manner. The delicate whorls of her ear captivated him.

He leaned close and felt the stirring of her breath against his own skin. Apple blossoms came to his thoughts, those sweet petals carried away with the wind in the springtime on the hillsides.

Her words were a strangled whisper in the small room. "I still think I have to be imagining all this."

Wildon lifted her chin and thought the perfection he saw in her features so delightfully unique that never again in all the millennium would another face come even close to the one he held so tenderly in his hand.

The spellbinding tempo of the Sidhe music intensified and a sudden rush of wind warned him that they were to be no longer alone. Enid appeared--and Tia's startled cry sent a new shaft of pain rushing to his heart.

"Hush. It is only my sister come with news, no doubt."

"But how did she get in?"

He heard the quiver in Tia's voice and saw the fear in her eyes. Clasping her hand in his, he gave her what he hoped was a reassuring smile.

"It is easy for the Sidhe to get in and out."

"No doors, no windows--people just morph in and out, except me."

He felt her erratic pulse and it worried him.

His sister, Enid, carried a small harp in her hands. Her long blond hair trailed behind her on the floor.

"You are beautiful, dear sister." She nodded to Tia and in one fluid motion swept into the jade chair.

Tia lowered her eyes and barely mumbled her thanks.

Wildon spoke to his sister in their own language. "She affects me like no other."

Enid wore a small, sad melancholy smile. "I have known the love of a human. They are fierce in their devotion."

"She does not want to remain with me." Saying it tore at him.

"You did not get her to drink the clover nectar?"

"No--I-I turned it into a snake."

Enid plucked a few strings on her harp. "Did you now? And was that to show her your masterful techniques in the art of love?"

Wildon frowned at her. "She was going to throw the chalice at me."

Enid gave a light laugh, a sound that captured all the merriment of tinkling bells. "Yes, human emotions are delightful. Such anger and such passion. You will not be bored ever again, dear brother."

Wildon frowned at his sister. "What has the council decided?"

Enid played the beginning of a Sidhe love tune. "You must go and talk to our father. I will keep your darling bride company."

"She is fearful." Wildon could feel the small hand in his turning colder.

"I know, but I will entertain her. You must hurry, brother. The king waits."

Wildon gave Tia's hand a squeeze. "I go to learn of the council's wishes. Enid will wait with you while I am gone."

He let her hand go. She nodded.

* * * *

"Your work with the humans has been a primary concern to us all. The council recognizes that the humans need proper guidance."

Wildon's father, the king, sat on a throne of gold, but the council hall had emptied. His father's voice echoed in the chamber. Wildon stood in front of his father, wishing he could tell him about the strong emotions he felt just being near Tia, but his father's eyes bored through him, dark and sharp. To his father, duty came first above all else and Wildon knew his father was assessing him.

"You must continue to belong to the environmental groups and attend their meetings. Your marriage can be beneficial to that end. Your human disguise will be less likely to be questioned and you will undoubtedly have the opportunity to place the appropriate spell on Angela Glenmore. Then we will have the chance of getting the proper legislation passed so that our home will be safe. "

"I've heard that Senator Glenmore has a very forceful intellect."

Wildon's environmental friends clued him in on the latest rumors. From what he had heard, he wondered if a common spell would have any effect on Tia's mother.

His father merely waved his hand. "Use one of the older potions then, they are the most reliable--even against inflexible personalities."

Some of Wildon's confidence returned. If he could prevent a nuclear power plant from being built above the Sifra, his efforts would always be remembered in Sidhe songs. He would be a hero.

"It is unfortunate that your new bride does not wish to remain here, but that can work for us as well. Return with her to her home. You must not stay more than a week or you will compromise your immortality and your powers, but that should give you plenty of time to change her mother. After a week, if your bride still will not return here, you must put a spell on her so she will not remember you."

"N-no!" Wildon sputtered. "I cannot make her forget me. Even if she will not return with me, at least she will always be haunted by my memory."

His father shot him a stern frown. "She might be able to

find the entrance to our home. That will not do. You will be free to marry a Sidhe maiden afterwards. You must remember your responsibility to your people."

A heaviness centered in Wildon's chest, but he nodded his assent. His father lifted up a green cloak and held it out to him.

"Here my son, you may go now."

"Yes, my father and my king." Wildon bowed and reached for the cloak. Within a moment he stood again in the small cell where Enid played her harp and Tia sat with her eyes staring straight ahead.

Wildon's throat felt tight. Enid had hypnotized his bride. It was the way of the Sidhe, but Wildon did not like it. Tia did not blink, and she barely breathed. His fine, fiery wife sat like a cold statue.

"She is ready for the journey." Enid lay the harp down and stood up. "Farewell, dear brother." She raised herself up on her toes and gave him a kiss of good-bye.

Wildon did not reply. He did not think he could control the sentiments that seemed ready to overwhelm him. He drew the cloak over his shoulders and lifted Tia into his arms. He looked down at his lovely woman and a great rush of wind swept them both away.

In the blink of an eye, he stood before a sign that read, "Glenmore Farms, Plant Nursery."

Wildon blew a gentle puff of his breath against Tia's cheek. She stirred in his arms.

"We are home, dear wife--you and I."

"What--where--I'm home?"

Tia lifted her head and blinked in the morning sunshine, but the effort of rising seemed too much for her. He gathered her even closer as he felt her lean back into his arms.

"What day is it?" She covered her eyes against the bright light of the new day.

"It is the morning after the night I found you." Wildon felt his heart grow in his chest. The rays of the light sparkling through the treetops above them set the orange glints in her hair ablaze with dazzling lights. "I can manipulate time, too."

"I remember being with your sister while she was playing the harp. Did I fall asleep? How did we get here?"

He shrugged. "It is easy for the Sidhe."

Tia shivered in his arms. "More morphing. I suppose it saves on gasoline."

"Indeed it does, dear wife."

"Please stop referring to our supposed marriage. I did not agree to it."

"I chose you, fair and lovely wife. We are bound together forever." He began to walk toward a quaint log cabin.

Her felt her deep sigh as she uncovered her eyes. She squinted at him.

"A green cape. Don't you think that's a little melodramatic?"

"It is the mantle of the Sidhe, a useful garment."

He felt her start as she glanced down at her clothing. The color rose in her cheeks as she ran her tongue along her dry lips. "My clothes ... I'm wearing my own clothes. Who dressed me? Your sister?"

He stopped at the bottom step of the small porch that led to the front door of the cabin.

"I did, my most beautiful wife. You are perfectly formed and far more exquisite than any treasure of the earth."

Excitement sparked in the air as her eyes grew dark, like the deep blue of the midnight sky when the moon is full. He watched the vein in her graceful neck begin to throb. Her lips took on the hue of bright partridge berries. He felt the heat of her skin on his own and his blood surged in a mad dance through his veins.

"Please put me down." Her tender mouth scarcely moved.

He knew she barely had enough air to breathe for he felt the same. The only breath he needed was hers.

"You are, to use another human expression, light as a feather, dear wife." He leaned closer to her lips. He watched her lashes flutter down against her cheeks. His senses, drunk with desire could hear nothing but the pounding of his heart.

Then someone grabbed his arm.

"Didn't you hear me! Put my daughter down, you big oaf!"

Wildon turned to see Angela Glenmore. He had seen many glamorous photographs of her with a bright smile, but she was not smiling now. She reminded him of a volcano ready to blow its top.

"How do you do, Mother Glenmore." He smiled as wide as he could but his misgivings concerning the imperious senator increased as he saw the orchid on her lapel vibrating.

"Don't you *dare* call me Mother! Put my daughter down this instant or I will call the police!"

She shouted in such a stentorian voice that Wildon winced. He gently placed Tia on her feet, but she swayed a bit so he held onto her.

"It's okay, Mom. He saved me from a carjacker."

"A carjacker! When? Why didn't you call me? I spent all night worrying about you. You didn't call last night and I knew something was wrong."

Angela Glenmore tried to snatch her daughter away from Wildon's supportive embrace, but he refused to let Tia go, especially since her legs continued to wobble.

"I couldn't call because my cell phone was in the car."

Wildon felt Tia take in a deep breath before she went on.

"And I--I passed out. Wildon revived me and brought me back here."

When Tia glanced up into his eyes, Wildon felt the delicate thread of desire binding them ever closer together.

He also caught the way Angela Glenmore narrowed her eyes and glared at him, measuring him from head to toe.

"Well, I suppose we owe him our thanks."

Wildon noticed the way she pursed her lips. He knew of a charm that would make her lips stay in that pose forever, but he restrained himself from casting the spell on her. He had--as humans liked to say--more important fish to fry. However, the thought occurred to him that if she did not look so appealing in photographs maybe some people would not vote for her.

"It has been my pleasure to care for your daughter. I've never met such an attractive woman. That's why I married Tia. I'm sure you'll want to be the first to wish us much happiness."

At that point, it sounded like Angela Glenmore was choking.

Chapter Three

Tia had spent most of her life living in her mother's shadow. Though she loved her mother, the constraints of being the daughter of a rapacious politician had more drawbacks than most people could possibly imagine. Tia had worked hard to set up her own business and to lead her quiet, calm life outside of the political arena. As she watched her mother sputter with rage, she had the sinking feeling that her serenity had come to an end.

"Mom, please, Wildon has a few peculiar ideas about life, but he's really a nice guy."

"He looks like one of those men on the cover of those dreadful romance novels you read, and that hardly makes him a suitable husband! What is his background? Does he come from a good family? Do you know what this could do to my campaign? Is he a Republican or a Democrat? Did you even think to ask? You are the daughter of the next president of the United States of America! How could you just run off and elope with this--this--this--eye candy!"

For some unfathomable reason, Tia began to laugh. Maybe it served to release some of the tension from her extremely weird experience. She had always tried so hard to be the dutiful daughter and the fact that her mother thought she had married Wildon simply because he was quite obviously a hunk struck her as hilarious. However, her laughter did not improve her mother's disposition.

"This situation is not funny! This is the absolute worst time for you to spring something like this on me. You could have waited--after the election we could have planned an elaborate affair."

Tia sobered instantly. "I have always wanted to avoid *your* spotlight."

It was an unfair outburst and Tia regretted it the moment it left her lips.

Her mother drew back as if Tia had slapped her. Switching

to an almost poignant tone and accompanying it with a beseeching look she said, "You used to be such a good child. It's all *his* fault!"

Tia's mother pointed a perfectly manicured nail at Wildon. "I will have a thorough background check done on you, sir!" she threatened.

"You can call me Wildon, Mother."

Tia glanced up into Wildon's jade eyes and found her senses stirring as if she had imbibed far too much wine. That was definitely dangerous. Dragging her gaze away, she turned to see her mother's face nearly purple with rage.

"Y-you can call me *Senator* Glenmore!"

Tia suspected her mother wanted to strangle Wildon with her bare hands. She would never do it, of course, because she might chip a nail and that would destroy her image. Her mother took great pains to appear poised and elegant at all times.

Her mother spun around and headed back to her waiting limousine. "Call me tonight! I will talk to the state police and order them to find your car and that carjacker immediately!"

Her chauffeur hurried to open the door.

Tia let out a ragged sigh of relief as the car pulled back onto the road.

"Easy come, easy go," Wildon commented.

Tia shook her head. "Wrong idiom. That one refers to money--not mothers."

"Oh." Wildon simply shrugged. "I do get them mixed up sometimes."

Tia gnawed at her lower lip as the cloud of dust from her mother's vehicle dispersed in the sunlight. "I've never seen Mom in such a state. It must be the stress of the campaign. Please don't be upset with her."

"You love her very much."

His eyes grew darker with a serious look that Tia found oddly disconcerting. Until that moment, she'd thought of him only as selfish, greedy, and frivolous. She hadn't suspected he had a solemn bone in his body.

"She's my mom. We had some rough years when I was a teenager, especially after my father died. I became a bit rebellious, but she's been a good mother all along. She's always been there for me." Tia's eyes grew misty as she remembered her mother nursing her through a bout of the flu and her last heartache.

Wildon drew her closer. She had almost forgotten that she had been sheltered in his embrace all this time, but now with her mother gone she found a flare of desire springing up from deep within her.

He gave her the most endearing smile and she found it nearly irresistible. The fire inside her glowed hotter and she knew she had to put some distance between them. She placed her hands up against his chest, but instead of pushing him away, she found the feel of his hard chest started a tremor inside her.

"You must yield, my sweet wife, and let the passion unfold for us."

Tia blinked. Had he hypnotized her? With her last ounce of reason, she broke free of his arms.

"We do not have a legal marriage in this state." She could barely mutter the words. She stumbled up the steps to her front door. Then she remembered that she didn't have the key. It had been left behind in the car, on the same ring as her car key.

She leaned her head against the door and closed her eyes. She debated whether she should just kick the door or call a locksmith.

"Is this what you need?"

Tia opened her eyes. Wildon had his hand open, and in the center of it lay a key that looked exactly like the one that fit the lock. She reached for it, but he closed it up in his fist.

"A kiss, dear wife, first."

Tia glowered at him. "That's blackmail."

"Let's call it friendly persuasion."

"I don't even know you!"

"We are married, it doesn't matter."

Tia ground her teeth together. She had to get back into the house. She had a very important order to fill before one o'clock.

"A peck on the cheek," she stipulated with her hands clenched tightly at her sides.

He shook his head as a mischievous look came into his haunting green eyes. "Our first kiss must be special--and enthralling."

Her heart hammered against her ribs. "For that kind of a kiss, you've got to snap your fingers and make my car appear."

His generous mouth twisted upward into a wry grin. "For a vehicle that size, we must make love."

Tia's breath caught in her lungs. Despite his maddening arrogance, she could feel raw passion welling up inside her. Swallowing with difficulty, she glanced at her watch. It would take a few hours for her to fill that very lucrative order and deliver it. Who knew if he could really produce her car?

"J-just give me the key. Then you can kiss me."

"The kiss is first."

"All right!" she spat out. She stiffened and closed her eyes, steeling herself to endure his violation.

A few moments passed and nothing happened. Tia found herself growing anxious. She lifted one eyelid carefully and saw Wildon staring back at her with a long-suffering look.

"One must begin a kiss in the proper frame of mind. I have been kissing you with my eyes. Don't you want to kiss me with yours?"

Each of his words echoed mellow and deep, plucking at some vibrating strings in Tia's heart. At his sensuous suggestion, her cheeks grew hot. What was the matter with her? Why couldn't she resist his charm? Was it more magic? Had he manipulated her emotions?

"I-I have to get to work. I have an important order that must get out soon. Please, I need that key." Her voice had a breathy quality to it that surprised her.

Wildon merely lifted one eyebrow a fraction. "Business before pleasure?"

She found her knees growing weak. Mentally, she chastised herself. No doubt this foolishness *was* due to the fact that she'd read too many of those romance novels. Her mother had warned her from the time she was a teenager that reading those books would give her the wrong ideas about life--and particularly about married life. All the men she had ever dated fell short of her ideal--until now.

Her mother was right. He did look like the hero on the cover of a romance book.

"Okay. After all, I do owe you a great deal of thanks for saving me from that maniac--and getting me back here, safe and sound...."

She did not get to finish for his lips settled gently over hers. He tasted of fresh pine, late summer leaves, and the crisp air in the forest. As his mouth pressed with more insistence against hers, she found a new hunger possessing her and a need that left no room for reason. He drew her closer. In the shelter of his arms, the kiss became more intimate. She parted her lips for him and his tongue coaxed hers to an eager response.

Then from inside the cabin, she heard the phone ringing. At first, she didn't care, assuming that the answering machine would pick up the call. However, the annoying sound continued, warning her that she had forgotten--again--to turn on the machine. With an effort, she pulled back.

"I have to get the phone." She knew her voice sounded unsteady.

"Telephones are an annoyance."

She frowned at him. There was regret in the husky sound of his words and that surprised her. She assumed that only she had been affected by his enticing kiss.

He opened his palm and presented her with the key. She hesitated a moment before she snatched at it, but the phone kept on ringing.

Hurrying inside, she grabbed the phone. On the other end, she heard the voice of her lone employee.

"I've been trying to reach you, I hate to do this to you, but I have to quit."

Tia went numb.

"I got accepted into Yale, and I have to get things ready. Orientation is only a week away."

Tia leaned against the countertop as she felt the blood pooling in her feet. "You have to come in today. I have two hundred mums to deliver to the Serenity Resort. I can't do it all by myself."

"My boyfriend is taking me to New Haven and we're going to look for an apartment. He could only get today off. I'm really sorry."

Tia's hand shook as she hung up the phone. A cold sweat broke out on her forehead. She clung to the countertop as a sensation of weakness swept through her. "I don't feel too good."

Wildon caught her up in his arms and though Tia's head spun, she felt safe there.

"I will help you with your mums--but first, I think you need to eat."

"I can't understand it. I mean it is a shock that she quit but still...."

"It has been quite a while since you've eaten. I'm very sorry I didn't think of feeding you first. It is my fault, dear wife."

Tia looked up into his face. She saw his brow furrowed with worry.

"I ate lunch yesterday--I only missed supper last night and breakfast this morning."

"Time is different in the Sifra."

A dark chill went through Tia and she closed her eyes. She had been quite certain she had cracked a few ribs when she had fallen out of the car and she had injured her shoulder, too. However, when she woke up in the Sifra, her ribs and shoulder felt fine--as if nothing had happened to her at all. How many weeks did it take for bones to heal? How long had she lain on that satin bed in that filmy gown?

She opened her eyes and glanced up at Wildon as he laid her down on the sofa in her living room. His classic features had taken on a somber cast.

"You must rest. I'll prepare food for you to eat."

* * * *

Wildon opened a cupboard in the small kitchen and glanced at the array of boxes and cans. What he had tasted of human food pleased him. Humans tended to have a lot more variety in their diets than the Sidhe. However, he had no idea how to cook a human meal and since Tia needed sustenance soon, he didn't have the time to experiment.

He had forgotten how long Tia had slept in a state of suspended animation while she healed. Fear twisted inside him. His father had warned him that humans tended to be fragile. There were stories of humans kept too long in the Sifra who returned to their own homes and immediately crumbled into dust. Wildon shivered.

He picked up a box. On the back of the box was a picture of a nice looking meal, pasta primavera. He remembered eating something similar at a buffet hosted by the Sierra Club. He found another cabinet with dishes in it. Placing the dishes on the table, he concentrated on the photo and tried to remember exactly how pasta primavera tasted. Then he snapped his fingers.

One dish filled with pasta primavera. He repeated the procedure and filled up the second dish. He liked the colors in the food--bright green, vivid red, and a creamy white. He sniffed it and his mouth watered.

He found a carton of orange juice in the refrigerator. He filled up two glasses with the juice. He carried the food into the living room and placed it down on the low table next to the sofa where Tia lay. He saw the wariness in her eyes and felt a stab of grief. Why couldn't she love him as he loved her?

"This should stick to your ribs." He gave her his brightest smile, hoping to cheer her.

She lifted herself up on one elbow and her eyes narrowed. "I know I didn't have any broccoli or red peppers, or garlic for that matter."

"You had the box of pasta. That's all I needed." He took a fork and swirled the pasta around the utensil. He held it out to Tia. "Here, see if I did it right."

He saw the panic spark in her eyes.

"You just snapped your fingers to make this food. Didn't you? How do I know it isn't poison? How do I know it won't turn into a dish of s-snakes?"

He saw her shoulders tremble. Slowly, he put the fork back down on the plate. A tightness had come into his throat and he could barely swallow. "First of all, though I don't know how to cook the way humans do it, I do know what tastes good. I wouldn't ever poison you, dearest wife. I'm sorry about the snake, I shouldn't have done that. Anyhow, I wouldn't turn the pasta into snakes because I like pasta. Please, Tia, my lovely wife, you've got to eat."

"How long was I in the Sifra? In human terms?"

"Two months."

He saw her eyes grow huge with alarm. He fought against his own feelings of dread. He couldn't let her know the danger.

"You were sleeping," he explained. "You needed to rest to heal yourself."

"So the wedding was a dream."

"No. The wedding was real, though it didn't take long and you didn't need to expend much energy."

"What did you do? Hypnotize me? That still isn't right!" She turned her back to him and pounded the sofa cushion.

He remembered his sister's words. *Human emotions are delightful. Such anger and such passion. You will not be bored ever again....*

He lifted the glass of orange juice. "I didn't use magic for this. It came out of your refrigerator. Please, drink some of it."

"Go away."

Wildon set the glass down again. He sat on the floor and pushed his hand through his hair. Anxious and upset, he didn't know what to do, but he did know that humans didn't necessarily mean what they said.

Sometimes at the meetings he had attended, if there were too many bad feelings, one of the other members would tell a joke. The joke made everyone laugh and lightened the atmosphere. He had heard several of the funny stories, but he never did quite understand exactly what was so amusing about them. Still, he thought he could try one he had heard on Tia.

"A woman who was a tree hugger and had much money, lived in California. She also did not want animals to be killed-- so perhaps she was a vegetarian--and she bought some land with lots of trees, though there was one especially large tree on one of the highest points. The woman wanted to get a good view of her land so she climbed the big tree, but unfortunately she frightened a spotted owl who felt hc had to defend himself--after all it was his home and who could blame him...."

Tia groaned.

"I've heard that one and you are telling it all wrong."

"I am telling it exactly the way it was told to me," Wildon defended.

"You are injecting your own opinions."

"Well, of course! How would you feel if you were an owl and somebody came barging into your habitat...."

"You are barging into mine."

"You are my wife!" Wildon practically shouted at her. He

clenched his jaw tightly, but it didn't make the anger go away. He could feel his heart pounding faster, his breathing accelerating, and his skin growing hot. This sort of thing never happened in the Sifra. Was this what it was like to be a mortal?

"You married me against my will." She turned back to face him. "You are supposed to ask first."

"I am the son of the king!" He pounded the low table with his fist.

"I am the daughter of the next president of the United States."

Her cold look made his temper rise.

"Big deal!" he thundered.

"The first *female* president of the United States."

"How many humans would she have in her kingdom? My father rules over all of the Sidhe--and there are more than you can count!"

He clenched his jaw. She did not understand anything of the Sidhe or of his father's lofty status.

However, he suddenly found he didn't want to argue anymore. He wanted food--and he wanted it *now*. He must have expended a lot more energy than usual. He grabbed one of the plates of pasta. "If you aren't going to eat this, then I will. My plate and yours."

He proceeded to dig in with his fork. The first mouthful made him smile. "This is perfect. It is exactly the same as the food I had at the Sierra Club. I am a genius. You don't know what you're missing. This is absolutely the best stuff on earth."

She gave a little shrug to her shoulder.

"Garlic--I love garlic, a little olive oil, cream right from the cow...." Wildon twirled his fork around and stuffed his mouth with as much as it would hold. He sighed. "Oh, the carbohydrates. When I get hungry, I really need those."

He gobbled down another forkful. "I feel as if I could eat an elephant--"

"Horse is what most people say."

He noticed a touch of resignation in her tone.

"Elephants are bigger," he reminded her.

At that point, a surprising thing happened. Tia smiled--just a little, there was such a miniscule tilt to her mouth, but he saw it and it cheered him immensely. He stopped chewing for a moment as she sat up and lifted the glass of juice. A spark of joy warmed him as she drank some. Feeling a weight slide off his shoulders, he glanced at his plate of pasta primavera--which was almost gone--and took a welcome deep breath. Tia wouldn't crumble into dust. He looked up once more at Tia who now picked up her fork and pulled the other plate closer to her. He decided that humans were completely irrational.

"Are you sure this stuff is safe?" she asked.

It annoyed him that she should question his skills. He frowned at her.

"This entire earth is made up of the same material. It's all nothing but carbon chains. That pasta, that orange juice, me, you ... I only manipulated a few carbon chains to make this food. It's not brain science."

"But you can't boil water." She grinned as she stirred the pasta around with her fork.

"Why would I want bubbling hot water?"

"To cook pasta the ordinary way." She lifted a few strands of pasta to her mouth.

"Oh." Wildon smiled. He let out a huge sigh of relief. He had gotten her to eat something, and hopefully, she would be all right.

"You must show me sometime how humans prepare food."

"Mmmm." She swallowed the food. "You have to show me how to manipulate some carbon chains."

A heavy feeling descended upon Wildon as he watched her. It was one thing for a human to eat food created by a Sidhe outside of the Sifra, it had no ill effect on them. However, any human who ate food in the Sifra would walk around with glazed eyes and a simpering smile, in a dazed state of euphoria for the rest of their life--which would still be considerably shorter than the life of one of the Sidhe.

Wildon did not know if he could bear to see his lovely wife in a permanent trance. He sensed a well of passion in her and did not doubt it would far exceed anything the Sidhe knew of love. Romances in the Sifra tended to be brief. What passed for ardor in the Sifra had left him dissatisfied. He wanted more. He wanted depth and emotion--yes, even if he didn't always understand it, he wanted to *experience* it.

Nevertheless, if Tia did not come back to the Sifra with

him, he must obey his father and erase her memory of him. Then he had to live without her until the end of time.

He stared once more at his food. He didn't feel hungry anymore. He knew he had a duty to his people. Left to their own devices, humans could foolishly blow the earth apart. He was bound to do all he could to prevent that situation as well as to keep the whereabouts of the entrance to the Sifra safe.

In all probability, he had only a week's time to enjoy his new wife. He felt nearly suffocated by the thought of his bleak future without her. Until now, he never had a sad thought. The Sidhe did not tolerate sorrowful emotions in the Sifra and as he felt the dull ache of misery squeezing his heart, he decided that perhaps keeping the two worlds separate had been a good thing after all.

Struggling against the despair he felt, he acknowledged to himself that once he put a spell on her mother, Tia would most likely hate him anyway. She would certainly guess his part in the complete turnabout of her mother's political views.

He knew it could not be helped. Everyone in the Sifra would be counting on him. He was the son of the king.

Chapter Four

Tia watched as Wildon caressed one of the mums before he loaded it into her truck.

"I am very good with plants. I understand their language."

"Don't tell me, they use idioms, too." With perspiration dripping down her neck, she realized how sarcastic her words sounded. Resentment had her tongue getting sharper than usual. Wildon wasn't putting forth the effort needed to get the job done in a timely manner. He stood there calm and cool, stroking every mum before he placed it carefully in the truck while she shoved in five times as many mums as he did.

He didn't seem at all perturbed by her annoyance. He looked thoughtful. "Each plant, of course, has a different dialect but they all use a slow cadence, high-pitched, except for the trees."

Tia glanced up at him and felt that crazy tingle shoot through her. The man still looked like some kind of god to her, even without the tunic. He made her believe in fairytales. He even made her believe that plants talked.

"What about bonsai trees?" she asked.

His eyebrows rose. "I've never met any of those."

Tia stopped picking up mums and wiped her brow. She needed a long drink of water and the water cooler stood at the opposite end of the greenhouse, right next to the bonsai trees.

"Come along with me and meet my bonsai trees. Then you can tell me what their voices sound like." She could hardly believe she was having this conversation.

She led him through the greenhouse, past the cyclamens, the poinsettias, and the house plants, until they reached a small corner where she had an impressive display of bonsai trees.

Wildon's face lit up. "They are exquisite!" He caressed one miniature maple.

"Their growth is deliberately stunted." Tia held her cup under the spout of the water cooler. "It takes years to make them that way. I buy them from another nursery in Albany.

They sell like hotcakes when the holidays come."

"Sell like hotcakes?"

"That's another idiom. It means they sell fast."

"Oh."

She watched him touch the small pine next to the maple.

"I'm introducing myself." He told her with barely a whisper. "They are fearful, these dwarf trees. Such high voices, but they are old, and speak with wisdom much like the trees in the forest."

"Are they saying they're thirsty?" Tia poked her finger into the soil of one of the trees as she swallowed the water in her cup.

"No, they are saying you are truly a priceless bride, worthy of a king's son."

Tia nearly choked on the water. Nobody had ever used such elaborate compliments on her. It sounded old fashioned, but inside she nearly melted.

"I didn't hear anything," she whispered back.

"You must touch them." He lifted one of her hands to the leaves of a tiny holly. Her hand appeared slight cradled in his. Yet, he touched her gently, as tenderly as he lightly stroked the leaves of the small tree. "Be very still."

Tia found it difficult to breathe in a natural rhythm with Wildon so close to her. All the resentment she had felt while loading the mums into the truck vanished. Her heart thumped so loudly in her chest, she knew it would drown out the voices of the bonsai trees. She felt so intensely aware of Wildon that nothing else mattered. She could not deny the magnetism between them. It flowed like an electric current.

"They know we were meant for each other." Wildon softly breathed in her ear. A shiver of pleasure wound through her.

The phone rang, breaking the intimate spell. Tia shut her eyes for a brief moment in frustration before she went racing to answer. She assumed the call came from the Serenity Resort, furious that the mums had not been delivered on time.

It turned out to be her mother on the other end of the line.

"How do you spell that man's name?" she demanded.

Tia winced. She did not know how to spell Wildon's name--she did not know anything about him except that he had a knack for eliminating all her common sense.

"I'll get him on the phone, Mom. But first, you take a deep breath and calm yourself. I worry about you. You'll make your blood pressure go up."

Tia set the phone down and turned around, only to be startled to find Wildon right behind her. She had not heard him approach. He slid one hand around her waist with a familiarity that sent heat surging through her. Then he picked up the phone.

"Hello, Mother Glenmore. Nice talking to you again. Oh. My name. W-I-L-D-O-N. Yes. No middle initial. Forest. F-O-R-E-S-T. Correct. Lived here all my life. Is that all? Take care of yourself, Mother. Good-bye."

He hung up the phone and twined his other arm around her. "She doesn't trust me, does she?"

"I suppose she doesn't have a reason to do so." Tia's knees had the consistency of soggy pasta.

He kissed the top of her head. "Do you trust me?" Husky and sensual at once, his words carried a hint of challenge.

Tia hesitated. She knew she felt safe in his arms--but trust? Trust had to be earned. He had saved her from the carjacker, but then he claimed to have married her without her consent.

"We're just getting to know each other." She nearly cringed at her inane comment. However, it seemed the best she could do as the pulse of energy swelled within her, destroying coherent thoughts.

"Soon we shall be very accustomed to each other."

He swept his hands down her thighs and then up again. She thought she would collapse from wanting.

"B-but the m-mums." She stuttered, trying to regain her equilibrium.

"I put them all into the truck." He turned her around. "They were excited about going for a ride."

"When?"

"While you were talking to your mother."

She caught the faint mischievous light in his eye. She pushed him away.

"You zapped them there."

"I accomplished a task, quickly and efficiently, without wasting much energy at all."

She saw the stubborn set of his mouth and knew that

convincing him to do things without his magic would be hopeless. He stood there smug and proud and looking every bit the prince he claimed to be. He would be any woman's dream, but he had chosen *her*. She rubbed her hand over the creases in her forehead in an attempt to clear her head.

"Okay. Let's get going. At least the delivery won't be *too* late." She forced herself to pull her gaze away from him and thanked her lucky stars that nobody had been around to witness the mums move themselves into the truck. It would totally freak out her mother.

"Just one thing." She glanced back at him and felt the breathlessness return as his gaze locked with hers. "Promise me that you'll help me unload the mums in a tedious human manner."

He merely lifted one eyebrow studied her with his jade green eyes. Her heart did a crazy little dance.

It took all her strength to swing around and get back to the truck. Surely, he had wound a spell about her.

* * * *

Wildon remembered the words of the bonsai plants as he stood in the greenhouse by himself hours later. He had not told Tia all of the things that the wise dwarf trees whispered to him, but the afternoon with Tia had gone so well, he had hopes to accomplish what the bonsai trees had suggested. However, first he had to prepare a special infusion for Tia's mother.

He draped the green mantle over his shoulders while he thought about the time he had spent with Tia. He admitted to himself that it had been fun. He hadn't expected that helping her unload the mums at the resort the hard way, with his hands, would give him any pleasure but Tia had rewarded him with smiles that completely captivated him.

On the way back, they had stopped in a small shopping center where Tia had bought some food. Humans had a rather laborious system for acquiring food in his opinion, but the process did offer an informal social gathering. Tia introduced Wildon to some of the people she knew in the store. She did not present him as her husband, but her cheeks blossomed into the most becoming shade of rose he had ever seen. Tia's acquaintances seemed surprised by his presence.

Wildon glanced around the greenhouse. Not even the cyclamens could match Tia in beauty and grace. She was, as the bonsai trees had told him, truly worthy of a king's son. He felt a deep sorrow stab his heart for the deceit he must carry out toward her mother, but it could not be helped.

Tia had insisted on making him a home-cooked meal. He had told her that he would water the plants in her greenhouse while she cooked. That gave him time to gather the ingredients he would need for the potion he must make.

He had merely snapped his fingers to get the watering job accomplished, but gathering the necessary items for an ancient infusion required a few complicated maneuvers. He whirled around and with a rush of wind he transported himself deep into the earth. There he set about acquiring all he would need to transform Angela Glenmore into an anti-nuclear activist.

It took him far longer than he had anticipated to formulate the special brew. Then he had to manipulate the time to reappear in the greenhouse only a few minutes after he left it.

The covered quartz container in his hands brimmed full of the frothy liquid he had concocted. Highly unstable, the fluid needed to be kept cool. The best place would be Tia's refrigerator where he could easily slip a few drops of his potion into anything that Angela Glenmore drank or ate when she came to visit. It wouldn't take much--just a few small drops. The results would be instantaneous, unless Angela Glenmore had a heart of stone, a distinct possibility judging from what he had seen of the senator.

Gingerly, he set the quartz container down on a counter in the greenhouse. Taking off his mantle, he folded it carefully and placed it in his backpack. Then he gently lifted up his potion again and walked with caution to the cabin where the aroma of garlic being sautéed in butter wafted through the air.

Wildon inhaled a deep draught of the tempting scent and felt his stomach rumble. No one ever used garlic in the Sifra, but he had found it a delight and another reason that he enjoyed visiting the human world.

At the door of the cabin he stopped. He had to disguise the unusual container before he slipped it into Tia's refrigerator. He gave a slight curve to his index fingers and suddenly he had what looked like a bottle of wine in his hands.

Stepping into the cabin, he found Tia laboring over the stove with her back to him.

"The watering didn't take you very long. Are you sure you did a thorough job?"

"I asked the plants first if they felt they needed water. They said sometimes you give them too much." He opened the refrigerator and hurriedly slid the bottle as far back as it would go. Then he put a bottle of milk in front of it. He thought of making the potion completely invisible, but then he might not be able to grab it readily when he needed it. He realized he could have precious little time to add the potent elixir to Angela Glenmore's food. He moved a bottle of ketchup in front of it for good measure.

"So now the plants are complaining about the care they receive?" she asked.

He closed the refrigerator door, but he furrowed his brow with worry. Should he stand guard by the door?

"Your plants are happy enough. However, they think they would be happier outside."

She chuckled. The short, merry sound thrilled Wildon. He smiled as a renewed sense of hope wound through him. He forgot about watching over his potion. He wanted only to enjoy his beautiful woman.

"My poor little innocent plants." She sighed. "They are far safer in the greenhouse. The real world is full of danger."

Wildon came up behind her. Settling his hands on her waist, he kissed the top of her fiery head. He felt the shiver run through her and knew that they would share a pleasure that would more than satisfy them both.

"From now on, I will watch over you so that no more danger can come close to you. Would you like me to turn that carjacker into a toad? It would please me, dear wife."

She turned to face him, her sapphire eyes had a hint of fear in them. "Could you really do that?"

He sobered for a moment. "Toads *are* complicated, one slight slip of the wrist and he could turn out to be a fish. Would you rather I turn him into a cockroach? Or a grasshopper? Tell me, my lovely bride, that I might please you."

She gave a shrug and went back to stirring the sizzling

food in the pan. "That man should be prosecuted in the courts and put in jail so he doesn't hurt anyone else."

"If I turn him into a toad, he won't hurt anyone else. In fact, he may become a snake's dinner. If I turn him into a cockroach, there's a very good chance that he would be crushed by someone's foot."

He heard her sniff and saw a tear run down her cheek. He floundered as dismay crushed the brief spark of joy he had felt.

"Why are you sad? What has hurt you?"

He wiped away the tear, but the dampness still lingered on her cheek.

She shook her head. "I was *so* scared. Let's not talk about it. Okay? Why don't you fill the wine glasses? There's some wine in the rack at the end of the counter." She pointed in the direction with the spoon in her hand. "I think the Merlot would be nice."

Wildon felt a cold knot twist in his stomach at the mention of wine. Maybe he should have changed the quartz container into something else less appealing to the human palate than wine.

Ice spread through him. Too much of that elixir could mentally disable a human. He gave Tia a brief squeeze and walked back to the refrigerator. What food did many humans dislike?

He opened the door to the refrigerator, moved the ketchup and the milk and briefly touched the wine bottle. It became a large can of anchovies.

"The wine is in the rack. What are you doing in the 'fridge?"

"Getting ice cubes."

"Those would be in the freezer--the top door."

"Oh. I'm still getting used to this mechanical stuff."

Wildon closed the refrigerator door and searched through the wine rack for the Merlot. He frowned at the cork stuck in the top of the bottle. Why did humans always have to do things the hard way? He flicked his thumb and the cork flew out.

Tia's small table had already been set. Pouring the wine into the stemware glasses, Wildon contemplated the suggestions of the bonsai plants. Basically, they had told him to seduce his wife. In the Sifra, seduction would have been simple, but--as usual--in the human world, nothing was ever easy. Even for the son of the king. How could he lure his own wife into intimacy with such a poor setting?

He filled the glasses to the brim and looked at the table. It needed some ambiance. He glanced down at his flannel shirt and jeans. Human clothing tended to be so restrictive. Not an inch of his skin was showing.

He knew using his Sidhe skills to manipulate objects had a propensity to anger Tia, but she was his wife. The wife of a prince. Daughter-in-law of the king. He flexed his fingers and studied the table. How could she possibly object to gold chalices instead of simple glass? Why would she dislike a damask tablecloth? He narrowed his eyes and glared at the flatware. No. Tia deserved sterling silver!

He fisted his hands and then threw them open with as much force as he could. Bright white light exploded through the small cabin. He heard Tia scream.

"What have you done?" she cried.

Wildon saw her shaking in terror and struggled with uncertainty. Had he gone too far?

"My dear wife, you are the bride of a Sidhe prince. You deserve to dine in the grandest manner." He went to her, but she held out the spatula in her hand as if she might slap him with it.

"M-my table, my glasses--everything looks like a Rococo nightmare. Y-you're in that tunic again and I look like a Grecian goddess in this outfit. I thought I was awake all this time ... but maybe ...." She covered her eyes. "Maybe if I just lie down for a while, I'll wake up and everything will be normal again."

Wildon stared at the spatula. He didn't dare turn it into something else. He cooed softly, as though he were talking to doves. "This is our wedding night. I wanted to make it special for you, my extraordinary wife. You are more beautiful than any other. This is to be a night of love."

She took the hand away from her eyes.

"Okay. This is all a dream anyhow--although I am really hungry...."

Deep ridges seemed drawn into her forehead and Wildon wanted to smooth them out. He wanted his wife to be joyful for he knew that most humans simply worried themselves to death. He held out his hand.

"Come, my fair bride, let us eat our fill."

"Good idea. Why don't you just zap the food out of the pan and into our dishes?"

"If it will please you."

"It will please me if I don't have to clean up the pots, pans, and dishes later, too."

"You will never have to wash those things again. I promise."

"You've got a deal."

Wildon casually waved his hand and the golden plates on the table were piled with the food Tia had prepared. He snapped his fingers and the stove and sink sparkled with a clean shine. The pots had disappeared.

"I hope you put the pots back where they belong," Tia commented.

"Everything will be exactly as it was."

* * * *

Tia could not quite reconcile herself to the idea that she lay in the midst of a deep dream. Everything seemed too solid and *real*--especially the sensations that spread through her with every touch. During their dining experience, the urge to make love with Wildon nearly consumed her. He sat next to her, pressing his bare thigh against the wispy fabric of her gown. Her own naked feet could not seem to stop toying with his. Though the gleaming sterling lay on the table, he used his fingers to lift a piece of broccoli to her lips. He teased her with it before allowing her to close her mouth around it, and when she finally had it in there, she found Wildon's finger had slipped in as well. She couldn't chew on his finger and she couldn't talk. Slowly, he drew his finger out, then he slid it along the sensitive flesh of her lips. A shiver of anticipation ran through her.

Anxious, she gave a small laugh. Wildon's face had seemed curiously intent until that point, but her nervous giggle brought out the sunshine of such an engaging smile on his face that her heart turned over. Deciding to play his game, she lifted up a sliver of sweet red pepper and poised it near his lips. He opened his mouth and she placed her offering carefully on his tongue. Then he closed down upon the sweet pepper and her finger. As he twirled his tongue around her finger, she realized that she was trapped by a whirl of emotions that she could not control.

Piece by piece, they fed each other until the diversion became an obsession and they forgot all about the food. Their lips met, and the kiss nearly drained Tia of reason. She clung to Wildon, wanting him to devour her with his hungry mouth. His lips slid downward, slowly tasting her neck. His hands drew away the top of the gown so he could explore the tender valley between her breasts with his tongue. As the moist heat of his lips pressed against even more sensitive skin, she moaned aloud.

Then the phone rang--though it took her a moment for that fact to register in her lust-drugged consciousness.

"Ignore it," Wildon whispered as he drew her against him. His breathing sounded ragged and she felt his heart pounding in time with hers.

"No, it's probably Mom ... again...." Reluctantly, Tia pulled away from him. "If I don't answer, she'll send her posse over here."

"Posse?"

"The local cops."

"You aren't doing anything wrong."

Wildon lowered his head to kiss her again, but she slid away from him while the phone kept ringing.

She stumbled to the phone and picked up the receiver.

"Hi, Mom." She found she could not control the breathy quality of her voice.

"The police found your car."

Tia froze. Attempting to remain calm, she asked, "Is it okay?"

"It's totaled."

"And the carjacker?"

"They haven't found him yet, but they *know* who he is. It wasn't a random carjacking."

Tia heard a slight catch in her mother's voice and felt a chill shiver up her spine.

"You cannot stay there tonight!" Her mother sounded near hysteria. "The nut who carjacked you is one of those crazy tree huggers. He's been sending me hate mail on a regular basis. I just received an email from him an hour ago. He knows where you live and he intends to--to hold you hostage."

Chapter Five

Tia pressed her lips together. Her mother's ambition had caused this predicament. How much worse would it become when her mother succeeded in reaching the White House?

"You don't have to worry. I'm not alone. We were just finishing dinner."

"I seriously doubt whether that stud muffin husband of yours would be any good at protecting you!"

Tia glanced at Wildon and felt her insides melt into a puddle of need. He arched his brow as he stared back at her. His skin glowed in the candlelight from a sheen of perspiration. She pressed a hand against her own fevered cheek and knew how much she wanted him. He had saved her from the carjacker once. She wasn't worried. She just wanted him to continue kissing her.

"We'll be fine, Mom. I'll check all the locks ...."

"This man has a rap sheet as long as the Thruway!"

Tia's mother screamed so loudly that Tia had to hold the phone away from her ear. Wildon got up from the table.

"May I speak with your mother?"

Tia handed him the phone. He took the phone with one hand, but with the other he drew her up against him.

She closed her eyes and reveled in the feel of the man in her arms. This hunger had to be madness--but she didn't care any longer. Her hands slid along the skin beneath his tunic. His voice rumbled above her, but she didn't pay much attention to his words. She touched the hard angles and taut muscles, splaying her hands across his broad chest and narrow hips, she memorized each incredible inch of him.

"Yes, Mother Glenmore. I understand the problem ... no ... you should not worry ... I realize that ... we can make other plans ... of course. I know a place where we'll be perfectly safe."

The click of Wildon hanging up the phone startled her and she opened her eyes.

"It's all settled," he said.

"What?"

"We'll spend the night in the forest. He'll never find us there."

Tia's heart nearly stopped.

"No! I am not camping out! Besides, there are bears out there and--and *snakes*--and creepy bugs."

With an air of supreme confidence, Wildon traced a line from her chin to the cleft of her bosom. "For you, there will be nothing but passion." Then he kissed her once more and she found his tender promise easing away some of her misgivings.

* * * *

An eerie chill crept up Tia's spine as she locked up the cabin. Night had settled all around her. Until now, she had never been afraid of the darkness, but her mother's warning had her on edge. Every breeze rushing through the trees and every chirp of the crickets made her jump.

Wildon refused to tell her anything about his special hideout, but he told her she could bring along some food if she liked--not that it was necessary, he assured her. Still, she knew he might just whip something up with a wave of his hand otherwise, and somehow she felt better eating food that had gone through the slow process that started from a seed. Maybe because she was a horticulturist growing things seemed enough of a miracle for her.

She lifted up the bag she had packed and came down the steps of the porch.

"Do you have some straw?" he called out to her as he peered through the glass of the greenhouse.

"Why don't you snap your fingers and create some?" She made no attempt to hide the edge in her voice. She felt angry that she had become a target of a maniac because she happened to be related to Angela Glenmore. Her life was being turned upside down due to her mother's grand designs. The insanity of it grated against her raw nerves.

As she drew closer to Wildon, her insides began fluttering. Her anger dissipated.

"There are certain manipulations that call for basic

ingredients." He gave a casual shrug. "It's like a recipe. I need but a few small pieces."

"What are you making?

"A special wedding gift for the beautiful wife of a Sidhe prince."

She had to admit that she was beginning to enjoy his odd compliments--even if they seemed somewhat chauvinistic.

"There are several bales of hay in the shed." For a moment, she wondered if he would give her a diamond tiara, or maybe a stunning necklace made of emeralds.

However, as he left her to stroll off to the shed at the side of the greenhouse, she shivered; it was as if he took the warmth with him. She studied the fluid movement of his athletic physique as he walked away and found it set her pulse racing once more. Hiding out for a night with him could be heaven, if she wasn't scared half to death. She thought once more of the carjacker and his threat. Peering anxiously down the road at the headlights in the distance, she wondered if changing her name would be effective in preventing future threats.

What if she really was Mrs. Wildon Forest? The thought brought a smile to her lips. Wildon defied logic, but perhaps that was exactly what she needed at the moment. Her carefully ordered life was unraveling and she had to admit that Wildon was a welcome distraction.

She went back to the porch and sat down on the steps, hugging her arms tightly about her. She did not want to be paranoid for the rest of her life, suspicious that everyone was out to get her, but she realized that her own personal peace would cease to exist if her mother became president.

A sudden, unfamiliar noise startled her and she gripped the porch railing as every nerve coiled tightly, ready to spring. When she heard the sound again, her breath caught in her throat.

Then Wildon's voice floated to her on the evening breeze. "You are a fine steed, as majestic as any in the Sidhe realm. Tonight you will carry my lady and I to our wedding bower."

Tia turned to see Wildon leading a gigantic white horse whose coat gleamed in the moonlight. The sheer size of the beast intimidated her.

"W-where did that horse come from?"

"The straw, of course." Wildon patted the animal's neck. "Horses are very easy for the Sidhe. It is the finest gift I could give to my beautiful bride, the only one truly fitting of her status as my wife."

Tia gulped. She had never owned a horse before, much less ridden one.

"We could just use my old truck."

"We are going where there are no roads."

"B-but, we'll get lost!"

Wildon's rich laugh echoed in the stillness of the night. "The Sidhe never get lost."

Tia looked up at the huge dark eyes of the horse. "Can horses see well in the dark?"

"Do not worry, my beautiful wife, I have lived here all my life. I know the way. Come, I will help you mount this fine creature."

Wildon gave her a leg up onto the bare back of the horse. If the horse had been the least bit skittish, Tia would have panicked and begged to get off, but the horse remained calm and steady. Without the least effort, Wildon joined her on the horse.

Wildon's arms held her close. "You see my love, this is far better than riding in your truck."

Tia's pulse leaped as he caressed her lightly before urging the horse into a gentle canter.

Leaning back against Wildon's solid chest, she closed her eyes as the rhythm of the horse's gait and the warmth of Wildon's arms chased away all the anxiety caused by her mother's dire warning. The sparks of desire flared up once more in her until she felt breathless. The night did not seem so menacing anymore. She looked forward to reaching the hideout where she and Wildon would share a night of love and passion, her magical night with her magical prince--as in the fairy tales she had adored as a child--as in the romances that she read now as an adult.

A chill breeze whistled through the heavy woods and Tia opened her eyes to see an unfamiliar path ahead of her. A sudden cloud of unease threatened to grip her once more when the thought of tomorrow loomed in the future. Would her story have a happy ending? Would her magical prince disappear into the fog that had originally brought him to her side?

She tried to turn to see his face, but the shadows were deep under the canopy of night.

"Will you really stay with me--forever?" she asked.

"I have chosen you and you are my wife," Wildon stated in his simple manner.

"Yes ... but will you be ... faithful?"

She felt the quick tightening of his muscles.

At that moment, a bright light flashed on and a man shouted at them.

"You won't escape me this time, Tia Glenmore! Get off the horse and nobody gets hurt, otherwise I put a hole in you."

Tia's insides turned to ice. She could not mistake the voice of the madman who had terrorized her. He came closer, shining the glaring beam of a halogen lamp directly into her eyes. She held her hand up to block the brightness.

"You heard me. Move! Who's with you? Your bodyguard? One wrong move, mister, and you're history!"

"Frog or cockroach?" Wildon whispered in her ear.

"I don't want no conversation! I'll blast your head off!"

"Perhaps a worm, it would suit him," Wildon commented.

At the sound of the gun blast, Tia screamed and the horse reared up. Tia fell to the ground, still held in Wildon's arms. The landing took the breath out of her, but Wildon had hit the ground first and taken the brunt of the impact. Dazed, Tia tumbled away from Wildon and sat up. She realized that the horse had vanished. Trembling with panic, she turned and found that Wildon lay still. In the harsh gleam of the madman's lamp, she could see blood splattered across Wildon's face and neck.

"No!" Tia cried. "You can't die! You aren't supposed to die! You're supposed to live forever!" The tears welled up in her eyes as she brushed the golden strands of hair from Wildon's bloodied brow.

"I *saw* the horse," the madman mumbled. "It *was* there. Right there. I shot it."

Tia glared at the evil monster who stood with his back to her. The wicked man stared at the ground, aiming his light at a small pile of hay.

Fueled with anger and despair, Tia hoisted a fallen branch

from the ground and got to her feet. Holding the branch over her head, she aimed it directly at the man's cranium and let him have it.

He crumpled to the ground.

She fought against a sudden wave of dizziness. Letting out a sob, she sank down on her knees besides the carjacker's inert body. She had never deliberately hurt anything until now. She didn't even swat flies. However, this horrid man had killed Wildon--her beautiful, amazing prince.

"Did I ... black out ... or something?"

At the sound of Wildon's unsteady voice, Tia jumped. Shaking badly, she swung around and saw him sitting up with a stunned expression on his face.

"I thought you were dead! I thought he had killed you!" She grabbed the carjacker's lantern and rushed to Wildon's side.

"No, no--dead, that's ridiculous." His brow furrowed and he muttered. "But I guess I did pass out. Very odd. Usually after a week there are signs, one might even say unmistakable warnings but this--so quickly. Strange."

He made less sense than usual. Tia bit her lip and tried to keep her voice calm. "We have to get you to a hospital."

"Hospital! By the blessed sprites! Don't ever put me in one of those places! I'm not hurt ... well, much ... but that maniac shot that beautiful steed!"

"He shot you, too. You're covered in blood."

"That is horse blood." Wildon snapped his fingers and the blood on his face vanished. "How long was I out?"

Tia blinked in surprise. Her fingers quivered as she reached up to touch the chiseled planes of his face where the blood had been. Not a single scratch marred his perfect skin.

"It wasn't long, a minute or so." A sudden wave of horror coursed through her. Her body chilled and she felt herself go pale.

"I ... I clobbered that creep because I thought he had killed you."

Wildon's smile beamed down upon her and for a moment she felt lost in his amazing jade eyes. "My wonderful wife, you are such a fierce lover."

"But ... what if ... I *killed* him?" Tia trembled as she turned to look once again at the carjacker's still form. Her stomach tightened into a cold knot.

"Do not fear, my precious wife. He is not dead."

"How can you be sure? I-I hit him as hard as--" She could not choke out the rest.

"He breathes. His heart beats. His soul stirs with energy. Do you not sense it?"

Tia stared at the fallen form and shook her head.

Wildon drew her into his arms. "Perhaps it is just another skill of the Sidhe that humans do not seem to have developed, but in truth he is not hurt badly. Though a bit more addled than before, he will soon be up to his old tricks again. However, I can still turn him into a worm if it would please you."

She savored the warmth of his embrace, burying her face against his throat. Tears welled up in her eyes. Only a minute before she thought she had lost him forever.

"I want him to be prosecuted in the courts."

"He could spend the rest of his very short life eating dirt as a worm."

"But nobody would know it," she sighed. "If he goes on trial and gets a stiff sentence, some other fool may think twice before he attempts to kidnap the relative of a political figure."

"From what I have observed, there are legions of humans willing to risk incarceration or death just to become famous themselves. Your legal system is not a deterrent. If I change him into a worm, there is no story--hence, he does not become a legendary hero for some other misguided activist to imitate."

She clung to him while his breath fanned warmth against her cheek and stirred up small sparks of desire.

"My mother would not believe me if I handed her a worm."

Tia could almost picture the scenario in her mind. A light laugh bubbled up inside her.

"Mom absolutely abhors worms."

"He could 'worm' his way into her confidence." Wildon's laugh joined hers.

For some reason, his words seemed so much funnier than the situation warranted. Tia found herself laughing so hard that tears she had tried to hold back now streamed down from her eyes. Wildon gathered her closer and appeared to be as sincerely amused as she was.

"Perhaps he could 'worm' some political information out of her," Tia joked.

"I've heard it said that even a worm will turn," Wildon added.

Tia sobered. "I sure hope this worm gets his just reward."

"Isn't it said that the early bird gets the worm."

Tia drew back and cast another glance at the fallen criminal. "I guess we should tie him up. I want him to be locked away as soon as possible."

"Such a detail would spoil our night of passion."

She heard the huskiness in Wildon's voice and studied his face. She could not mistake the glint of eagerness she found there, and though she longed to lose herself in a fantasy, the reality of the situation would not allow her heart to do so.

"But we can't just leave him here. He'll get away."

"True." With a grave sigh, Wildon set her gently aside, stood up and walked over to the prone man. Tia frowned and got to her feet as Wildon held his hands over the man. Wildon clapped twice and where there had been a man, a rock appeared.

"There. He won't go anywhere now."

No matter what kind of magic Wildon performed, it still frightened Tia. It defied the logic of the natural world and she couldn't help but think that somehow her own brain had played a trick on her.

Gingerly, she picked up the lantern and went over to the rock. When she poked it, it felt hard and cold, much the same as any other rock in the area--although it did have an unusual shape.

"Will you be able to change him back?"

"Tomorrow morning, if you like. Then you can tie him up and call the police. Right now, I must show you my special place."

"But your horse is gone."

"I still have my mantle."

He reached into his backpack and pulled out the green mantle. He draped it over his shoulders and reached for her.

"In my arms, you will be safe."

* * * *

She shut her eyes tightly as the wind whistled around her. Clutched closely by Wildon in the shelter of the green mantle, she felt weightless. However, within a moment, solid ground appeared beneath her feet.

"We are here." Wildon drew the cape away and released her. She found his method of traveling left her feeling rather lightheaded. Trying to get her bearings, she opened her eyes gingerly, but she was met only with the gloom of the shadowy nighttime forest. Thankful that she had taken the lantern, she turned it on. The bright beam sliced through the blackness and she gasped as she took in the surroundings.

"This is amazing." She saw steam rising from a rock pool nestled beside a waterfall. Adjacent to the pool, a green moss-covered ledge lay in the shelter of an overhang. Low pines made a natural fence which whispered in a breeze unusually warm for an August night in the Catskills.

"I've never seen anything so lovely. How far is it to the cabin?"

"There is no cabin. *This* is my secret hideaway."

She wanted to be angry with him for deceiving her, but before she could say anything, he began to unbutton his shirt. Her lungs constricted and her legs weakened. When the shirt fell to the mossy floor, she could do little but stare. The sight of his molded biceps, solid pectorals, and flat abdomen tailoring down into narrow hips started a strange aching in her limbs. Slowly, she sank down upon the luxurious cushioned moss. Mesmerized, she gazed in awe as he casually abandoned the rest of his clothing. Stunningly virile, he stood before her like a living, breathing Renaissance statue. Her heated blood throbbed wildly.

"I'm going to take a dip in the pool. Come join me, my lovely bride."

"I-I didn't bring a bathing suit." Her voice came out as a bare whisper.

"There is no need. We will not be disturbed." He twirled his right arm around and a heavy, white fog encircled them. The fog lay at the outskirts of the small enclosure and appeared to be impenetrable. However, within the circle of fog, the air remained clear.

"Come, my love, you will find the water a pleasure."

Her pulse seemed to be pounding in her throat. She put a hand to her neck.

"Do you need help with the buttons?" he asked, bending down beside her.

She blinked as if caught in a daydream, but Wildon did not appear to notice her confusion. Gently, he undid the buttons on her blouse--one by one--the hot tips of his fingers trailed a fiery path slowly downward until with a languid motion he drew off the cotton fabric. It lay beside his clothes on the spongy carpet of moss.

"Your hair must be spun of rubies and your skin of warmest opals." His hands cupped her face. His voice had a deep sensuousness to it that left her breathless. He brought his lips down on hers and time stood still while he coaxed her to a response that left her weak with wanting. She felt drugged as he removed the rest of her clothing, though he did it with infinite care and patience. She knew he could have simply clapped his hands and saved himself the trouble, but it seemed to please him to tease every inch of her. The intensity of her need spiraled wherever he touched her.

As he drew off her wispy panties, he seared her inner thighs with a blaze of kisses and she wanted nothing more than to draw him inside her, to feel herself filled with the passion he had promised would be hers tonight.

All her rational thoughts spun away. She begged him to end his torture, but he ignored her entreaties. He lifted her from the bed of moss and carried her into the rock pool.

She tensed, expecting to be shocked by icy water. Instead, she was immersed in warmth, a fact that surprised her. The mountain springs that fed the creeks of the Catskills usually carried the chill of the winter snow that had formed them, even in the summertime.

The light of the lantern suddenly dimmed and then went out. Tia shuddered as the entire area was swallowed up in total darkness. She clung to Wildon.

"There is no need to fear the night."

He lifted his arm and several lights appeared. They looked like glowing balls impossibly suspended in the air. Tia gazed at the soft radiance now surrounding her and her doubts returned. This fantasy of hers could not be real. The great desire nearly overwhelming her had to be some cruel trick of her mind. The unusual stress of the day must have left her with some strange psychosis. However, as she felt the heat of Wildon's body against hers, she could not deny herself the pleasure.

Wildon held her as he swam across the length of the pool. They floated on the gentle waves with his arm firm beneath her breasts and his full arousal brushing against the sensitive skin of her soft flesh, luring her body to meld with his. Hot rivers of desire spread through her.

Wildon came to rest against a smooth worn rock, drawing Tia upon his lap. The waterfall, only a few feet away, played a symphony of pleasant gurgles.

"My beautiful bride is troubled." Wildon brushed her ear with his lips and she quivered.

"Your magic scares me." She lowered her lashes. She was afraid to meet his gaze for she knew he would mesmerize her with his glorious eyes and she would never be able to voice her fears. "This whole scene could be an illusion--another one of your manipulations. You could be playing with my emotions--making me feel--so--so--well, I've never felt this way."

"It is wonderful. Is it not?"

"But is this real? Will I wake up tomorrow and find it only a dream?"

"There is no magic in the love between us. We are made for each other."

"At your command a thick mist encircles us. You raise your arm and lights appear in the air. It all seems like--like a fairy tale."

Wildon shrugged and began to stroke her most secret core. Tia moaned. Still a shred of her resistance lingered.

"We come from different races and different societies." Her words were almost a sob as she writhed with his masterful exploration.

"It matters little. When my heart beats, your heart echoes. I searched, but until I found you, no other in this world responded as you alone can do."

Could his claim be true? She laid one hand against his

chest and one hand on her own. Beneath her fingertips, she felt his heart pound out a rhythmic surging tempo that mirrored her own. Each pulse sent an electric jolt blazing through her.

"You see, my beautiful wife, we are in harmony."

Tia nodded. She lifted her gaze and fell into the wonder of his strange jade eyes. Then she abandoned herself to the gusts of desire and gasped in sweet ecstasy as they joined. Together, they swirled toward a passion that consumed them both.

Chapter Six

Wildon woke in pain. He groaned and touched the turtle-sized bump swelling in the area where his head had hit the ground last night as the horse reverted back into straw. Rubbing the tender area, he struggled to sit up and open his eyes beyond narrow slits, but the bright beams of the morning sunlight stung.

What had happened? He shoved at the blanket covering him and Tia. He had formed the down-filled comforter when they had finally settled in to sleep. That was the last thing he had manipulated before he closed his eyes.

Squinting, he glanced around him and his ancient Sidhe heart nearly stopped for he saw that his mist had vanished. A raw spurt of panic gripped him.

Between the ache in his head and the horror gnawing in his gut, he could barely think.

Tia stirred beside him and mumbled, "Come back to sleep."

"It's gone." His voice came out as a harsh croak.

"What?" she mumbled.

"All of it. Everything." He felt a tightness in his throat that he didn't understand, but he knew it couldn't be good.

He heard Tia give a long sigh. He stared at her as she stretched in the morning sunlight. She had been more delightful than he could have imagined. Their lovemaking could not have been more perfect, more fiery, or more exquisite. His soul had thirsted for an eternity until he found her. Now he wondered if the thirst could ever be quenched with just one taste of her nectar.

As she sat up, the blanket slid down, revealing her creamy breasts. He could feel the fire she had ignited in him smoldering.

"Everything looks like it's still here."

The seductive tilt of her mouth almost made him want to ignore his current difficulty, but the magnitude of his loss crushed any wayward ideas. He covered his eyes. He knew he could go mad.

"I have lost my ability to manipulate."

"You mean ... no more magic?"

He nodded. Simply the thought of it made the ache in his head intensify. He dropped the hand from his eyes and took a breath to steady himself. "Usually, it takes a week or more. However, it appears all my powers have vanished at once. Plus, I have this huge lump on my head and it is causing me a considerable amount of agony. I've never known pain. How can humans bear it?" Deep within, he felt a sinking emptiness grip him.

She frowned at him and it seemed as if a cloud passed in front of the sun. Then she got up on her knees to see the top of his head. Her breasts were mere tantalizing inches from his face. He remembered the taste of them, the pliable feel of each one. His excruciating headache seemed to recede a little.

"Hmmm. Nasty. You could have a concussion. We should get you to a doctor right away."

"Human doctors know nothing about healing."

"I can put some ice on it and give you a painkiller if you prefer." She plopped back down beside him and cooed, "I'll get you all fixed up."

A sudden, vengeful spasm shot through his skull. The bitter taste of mortality seemed more than he could bear. He lifted his index finger and pointed at a small clutch of leaves nestled against a rock.

"You see. Nothing!" His finger began to shake so he drew his hand into a fist and slammed it down upon the verdant moss.

He saw the confusion in her troubled eyes.

"What were you trying to do?"

"Make ice, of course." His words came out as a hollow echo while he struggled against his anguish and the throbbing torment in his skull.

"I have plenty of ice in the refrigerator back at the cabin. We'll get back there and cool down that bump." She scurried to the pile of discarded belongings and dug beneath the clothes until she found her backpack. "I brought along some fruit and cheese in my backpack. We'll eat and then head home. See, here it is." She held up the bag in triumph.

Wildon's body reacted rapidly to the sight of her slender, naked body; her long legs, flat stomach, trim waist, and firm breasts. He could hear the blood surging through his veins while he gazed at her faultless, unblemished skin glowing nearly translucent in the morning light. The sudden hunger that possessed him had nothing to do with food. He drank in every detail.

When she sat down beside him, she giggled and stared at the evidence of his lust. "I thought you lost everything." A bright flush stained her cheeks.

"I can no longer tweak carbon chains, but I am made of flesh and blood."

Her tremulous smile turned his heart over.

"Well, if your head isn't hurting too much, maybe you aren't hungry just yet."

"I will always be hungry for you." He drew her against him and forgot about his dire situation--even the affliction in his head faded. In every way, the love they shared there on the down-filled comforter seemed far more spectacular than what Wildon had considered perfect the night before.

Afterwards, they lay quiet for some time in stunned bliss, twined in each other's arms. Slowly, reality edged in and Wildon felt the weight of his misery wrapping itself around his joy. The bump on his head throbbed incessantly and reminded him that he had only one option.

They ate Tia's fruit and cheese. She had some bottled water with her as well. Wildon did not care about eating, but he knew he would need the strength for his journey.

They dressed in their clothes. Wildon stared out at the rock pool while Tia folded up the comforter. Strong emotions churned through him. The certainty of death rarely touched him. Some of the Sidhe had died in battle. Some simply grew beyond their time and passed away as his mother, the Queen, had done so long ago.

Had his fall damaged him? Had his fondness for human food weakened him? Had his love for a human robbed him of his power? Could his power be restored?

Tia slid her arms around him and gazed up at him with her wide, sapphire eyes, more beautiful than the placid water of the pool. He felt a tug at his heart. How could he leave his most precious bride? Yet, he knew he had no other alternative.

"I must return to the Sifra," he said. "I must consult with the wise ones."

She startled him when she pulled away from him and wrapped her arms about herself. With a short, acid laugh she, too, turned to stare out at the water.

"Sure. I knew this was all too good to be true. Nothing but a fairytale. And now I'm waking up and it will all vanish like a wonderful dream."

The catch in her voice nearly undid him. He laid his hand on her shoulder.

"I will come back as soon as I can."

She pushed his hand away and glared at him. He knew she didn't believe him.

"You are my wife!" He found his tone getting louder. "We are made for each other!"

"I'm just another one-night stand for you, aren't I? All you've got to do is sweet talk some other naive woman into believing that wife business and you're all set. How could I have been such a fool?"

She turned and walked away. "Don't forget your blanket."

Wildon found his temper rising. "I am the son of the Sidhe king!"

"Do you think I care?" She tossed the words over her shoulder.

Wildon was infuriated by her tone. "You will when you realize you're going in the wrong direction."

He watched her slow down and then stop.

"Just point out the right path."

"It is not a straight route."

She stamped her foot. "Why did I let you do this to me? Now everything is a disaster."

Wildon's anger faded. He felt as if he had a stone in his gut. "I did not mean for it to be so. I wanted it to be a perfect night of passion. One befitting the bride of a Sidhe prince. I wanted our love to be a legend--sung in the halls of the Sifra until the end of time. I did not know I would lose my power." Then he furrowed his brow and studied her. "Perhaps you have stolen it from me."

She whirled about with the blue fire flashing in her eyes and the color of hot summer roses on her cheeks. "That is ridiculous! Why is your magic so important anyhow? I don't care about your smoke and mirrors shenanigans. Why can't you just live like the rest of us?"

Wildon found himself frustrated with her lack of understanding and he lashed out at her.

"Because I'm not one of you! I am a Sidhe prince, son of the king!"

"You married me against my will in a questionable ceremony that will certainly not be recognized by the state of New York. To think that I was so naïve! Everything about you is as phony as a three-dollar bill!"

"A three-dollar bill?" Here was an idiom that Wildon had not heard before. "Please, explain that phrase."

"There aren't any three-dollar bills!" she shouted.

Wildon didn't understand at first why that should make any difference. "As phony as a three-dollar bill." He repeated softly, bewildered by the words.

"If someone hands you a three dollar bill, it has to be a fake--useless because it is not legal tender."

Understanding dawned on him and he clenched his fists as his temper rose. "Useless! I am a Sidhe, son of the--"

"Don't start that again!"

She held up her delicate hand and Wildon noticed that her fingers shook. He glanced at her face and noticed that her eyes were brimming with unshed tears. Again, he remembered that humans didn't always mean what they said.

Wildon sighed. He reached for her hand and heard her sniff.

"You know that I am not a fake." He said it simply, for the accusation had been ridiculous in the first place. "We are meant for each other. The bonsai trees knew it and after our lovemaking, there can be no doubt. You are sad that I must return to the Sifra."

"It was all so incredibly beautiful."

A tear rolled down her cheek and splashed on Wildon's hand. The small drop reminded him of the dew drops on the grass, but unlike the dew it held Tia's warmth.

"I am sad, too." Wildon kissed her hand, lingering over it

and giving it a slight squeeze. His throat tightened as he remembered the first time he touched her. "True magic lies in you and you do not know it. Your touch, the feel of your skin, the wonderful miracle that is you cannot be duplicated."

Her fiery hair glinted like red gold in the morning light and though it hurt his eyes, he did not wish to turn away from it. In truth, he did not know what would happen when he returned to the Sifra, especially since he had failed in his mission to convert Angela Glenmore to an anti-nuclear stance.

"I will guide you home, then I must find my way back to the Sifra--on foot. You must promise that you will not follow me."

"Why?"

He saw the curiosity in her expression and a chill of fear shimmered up his spine.

"You must not know the location of the entrance to the Sifra."

Her saw her shudder.

"You don't need to worry. I wouldn't *want* to go back there."

Her words did not reassure him. However, he had little choice but to trust her.

Together they walked back, hand in hand, toward her cabin.

Chapter Seven

A thread of anxiety wound through Tia as she stared at the man-shaped rock that used to be the carjacker.

"Are you sure you can't turn him back?"

"I am unfortunately as mortal as you are right now."

Tia bit her lip. "My mother will not leave me alone for a minute if she isn't certain that this guy has been rendered harmless."

Tia watched a shadow cross Wildon's face.

"He is still a danger. Somebody could trip on him."

A sad smile came to her lips at his comment. He seemed completely serious and she found his lack of artifice endearing.

They neared the cabin and she began to realize that the strength of her feelings for him didn't make much sense. She had never believed in love at first sight, but what she felt for him far surpassed any of her previous definitions of affection.

It wasn't all about their stellar lovemaking, either. It had more to do with the innocence she found in his face, the honesty in his answers. The way he always gave her the plain truth. His guileless knack for saying what he truly felt made her feel he would never lead her astray. She trusted him--and wasn't that what made a good match? Wasn't that what her father and mother had enjoyed? Absolute faith in each other? She knew Wildon wouldn't hurt her. She felt safe with him.

How many people fell in love in a day? She had always assumed that love had to grow and develop over time. How many of her friends lived with their boyfriends for years before they took the plunge and said their vows? How many of them had already filed for divorce?

She stole a glance at Wildon's classic face and frowned. Did he have a few lines around his mouth and eyes that had not been there yesterday? She studied him further and thought she noticed a few gray hairs woven in among the gold.

He turned to her and questioned her with his dreamy jade eyes.

"A penny for your thoughts."

She reached up and touched his cheek. "You look worried. I see some lines that weren't there yesterday."

He lifted her hand and brushed a kiss across her knuckles. "The pain continues unabated and I'm aging. I am wondering if I'll look like a human octogenarian by tomorrow. "

She saw the grim set of his mouth as misery stole across his features.

"I'll love you anyway." She meant it with all her heart.

Something flickered in the back of his eyes, but he gave her hand a tender squeeze.

Then the raucous sound of a car's horn drew their attention.

"You've got lots of company," he groaned.

Tia's heart sank at the sight of her mother's limousine, a police car, and another vehicle pulling up to the cabin.

"Please don't go yet--not until I get rid of them," she begged.

He gave her a forced smile that bore the unmistakable signs of his wretchedness. "I'll do my best to bore them with the same joke I tried to tell to you."

A bittersweet pain stabbed at her heart. She wanted to run off into the woods with him and forget about the rest of the world. How could she live without him even for an hour?

"Please, please promise me you'll come back." She could not hide the desperation in her voice.

"Yes, my sweet bride. I will do what I can."

Tia had no time to consider the note of uncertainty in his pledge. Her mother hurried to her to crush her in an embrace-- something Angela Glenmore rarely did because it would involve wrinkling her clothes.

"I worried about you all night."

"Wildon kept me safe."

Her mother totally ignored her attempt at reassurance.

"Last night was one of the longest nights of my life."

Tia pulled back and noticed that her mother did have dark circles under her cover-up makeup.

"Mom--everything was okay. Nobody bothered us at all."

Her mother handed her a cell phone.

"They found this in your car, surprisingly undamaged. It

has already been dusted for prints, but the only ones on it are yours. Thank heavens, we can keep in constant contact once more."

Tia stared at the cell phone in her hand. She wondered if she could call Wildon in the Sifra with it.

"Wildon tripped and hit his head on a rock. He needs some ice and some pain medication. Please excuse us for a few minutes." Tia nodded to the officer standing next to his patrol car and the other stranger before unlocking her door.

She winced when she saw the golden chalices, sterling silver, damask and the rest of Wildon's touches of ambiance.

Her mother, right at her heels noticed it, too.

"What is this Baroque nightmare?"

"Actually, I believe it is Rococo and it's Wildon's idea. Isn't he a sweetie?"

Tia could see that her mother was actually biting her tongue.

Tia filled a plastic bag with ice. Wrapping it in a soft towel, she insisted that Wildon sit down so she could place the makeshift icepack gently on his bump. She handed him a painkiller and a glass of water and stood over him while he took the medicine.

Tia's mother cleared her throat dramatically. "We have some things to discuss, dear, and I would prefer to talk with you in private."

Tia sighed. Wildon patted her hand.

"I'll be fine. The ice does help."

Tia and her mother walked into the greenhouse office. As soon as they closed the door, her mother started pacing the floor.

"First of all, let me tell you that the detective I hired cannot find a Wildon Forest listed anywhere."

Tia picked up the pile of mail on her desk and glanced idly at it as her mother went on.

"The detective's professional opinion is that Wildon Forest is a fictitious name concocted to cover up the truth behind the man's true identity. That man you call your husband is probably a crook or a con artist!"

Tia put her mail back down on the desk and laughed.

Her mother's mouth drew down into a frown. "I have hired

a bodyguard."

"Mom!" Tia stamped her foot.

"His name is Jacques and he was highly recommended to me by the governor."

"I do not need a babysitter! Wildon is not a crook. I trust him implicitly. He saved me from the carjacker." She would have liked her mother to know that he had saved her *twice*, but the evidence wasn't very convincing at the moment.

"You cannot judge a book by its cover!" her mother retorted.

Tia took a deep breath in an attempt to calm herself. "I realize that you are very concerned about my safety, but I have been taking care of myself quite nicely now for several years."

"But you are my daughter and with my candidacy practically assured, you need more protection. Of course, once I am the candidate, you will be able to rely on the Secret Service."

Tia clenched her teeth together. She hated the thought of going everywhere with an entourage.

"For now, I'll simply use Wildon's name."

"That cannot be his real name!"

Her mother's face grew florid and Tia's fury evaporated. Her mother's blood pressure could go dangerously high in a matter of seconds. Taking a deep breath and counting to three, she tried to get her mother to sit in a chair, but her mother was not about to let the matter at hand drop.

"You are too trusting! From the day you were born, I saw those big blue eyes of yours and I knew you were going to fall under the spell of some cunning con man!"

Tia pressed her lips together firmly. Yes, she had come under Wildon's spell, but she wouldn't have missed it for all the world.

"Mom, you've got to calm down. I'll get you something to drink."

Hurrying back into the kitchen, she found Wildon twiddling his index finger up and down while pointing at spoons that danced on the table. His bright smile dazzled her and turned up the warmth in her heart.

"Maybe the trauma from the head injury caused all the difficulty," he said. "The pain is gone and I can focus again."

Tia threw her arms around him and kissed his cheek. Gone were the creases and lines she had seen earlier. The lump on his head appeared to have diminished, though it hadn't disappeared entirely. She placed the ice pack back in place.

"Does this mean you'll stay?" A lurch of desire sprang up inside her.

"Your mother is angry." His forehead clouded.

"Mom thinks you're a crook and a con man." Twirling her finger around one of his golden curls, she gave him another kiss and felt a sizzle rush through her.

Wildon did not return her kiss.

"Your mother does not like me."

"I do and that's all that matters." Tia sighed. "But don't tell her that you're a Sidhe prince. She would have you committed to a mental institution."

"Indeed."

They both heard Angela Glenmore call to Jacques outside and Tia remembered why she had come back into the kitchen. She had to force herself to pull away from Wildon.

"I'm going to pour some diet cola for Mom. Would you like a drink, too?"

The spoons clattered onto the table and Wildon swung around. "I'll make up some tea." He rubbed his hands together and then clapped. A silver tea service appeared on the table. "You go along and sit your mother outside in the sunshine at the table on your deck and I'll bring out some little sandwiches like the ones I ate at the Sierra club. We'll get to know each other better and she'll feel more comfortable with me."

Tia rubbed her hand across her forehead. Unless Wildon produced a valid voter registration card, there would be little hope of changing her mother's feelings. If her mother caught Wildon in the act of tweaking carbon chains, it would be bound to create more havoc.

"Would you please use food from my refrigerator? I do have tuna fish, cheese, and bread. You don't have to whip up everything out of thin air."

"Do you have watercress?"

"Um--no. But I do have spinach. You can make a substitution."

"How about shrimp?"

"Tuna is cheaper."

"Garlic?"

"Mom can't take garlic."

"That is most unfortunate." He snapped his fingers and a dark green tablecloth appeared. He handed it to her. "You can cover the table with this."

Tia rolled her eyes. "It won't help. You shouldn't waste your time going overboard."

"Overboard?" He wore a puzzled expression.

Tia's headache intensified. "It's another idiom. It's an expression that came from boating, but it means you're being too extravagant."

"Overboard." His face brightened. "I'm going overboard." He rubbed his fingers together and clapped. A floral arrangement appeared consisting of mums, ivy, and baby's breath all gathered into a boat-shaped holder. "These are all from your greenhouse."

Tia blinked in amazement. She had seen some of the finest floral arrangements take shape, and this one ranked with the best. She reached out for it.

"I-I like it. It's really quite good. In fact, it's stunning. Where did you learn how to do floral arrangements?"

His brows lifted a fraction. "The Creator is the one who is the master at that sort of thing. All one has to do is take a walk in the woods and attempt to imitate what you see, though it is only a poor copy."

The baby's breath in the bouquet quivered as she felt herself caught up in his spell. His devastating appeal sent a tremor throughout her body. She saw his lazy smile grow wider as he noticed the effect he had on her.

"Run along, my dear wife. You and I will have plenty of time together later."

That thought sent a hot flush blazing on her cheeks. In happy anticipation, she hurried off to convince her mother to sit down for a while and join them for tea.

* * * *

"I'd like to introduce you to Jacques."

Tia's mother wore an implacable expression as she

motioned for Jacques to join them on the deck.

Tia resisted the urge to scream. She tried to quell the resentment building up inside her as she smoothed the tablecloth out and set the lovely arrangement in the center. She often wondered what had happened to the sweet mother she remembered from her childhood. All the wheeling and dealing in the political arena had altered her. She had become more than assertive. She reminded Tia of a steamroller ready to flatten everything in her path.

Straightening up, Tia decided she had to be equally forceful.

"It's nice to meet you, Jacques, but I will not need your services. Wildon has a black belt in karate." She clutched her hands together behind her back so her mother wouldn't be able to see how much they twitched, which always happened when she told a lie. Still, she reasoned with herself that if Wildon could turn somebody into a rock that did make him a formidable opponent.

Jacques merely nodded, but her mother's eyes narrowed.

"I will not spend another sleepless night worrying about you. That fanatic is still on the loose and remains a threat to you."

"Have you heard from him since yesterday?" Tia attempted to sound nonchalant, but she could not stop the edge of sarcasm in her voice.

"No, but that doesn't mean he isn't hiding behind some tree right now."

Tia's mother cast a worried glance out to the edge of the woods that bordered the nursery's property. Tia fought the urge to grab her mother's hand and drag her into the woods to show her the rock. That revelation could only make matters worse.

The sliding glass door opened and Wildon came out bearing the silver tray laden with a heaping mound of dainty sandwiches, plates, cups, and teapot.

Tia caught the gleam in his eye and took in an unsteady breath. She could feel herself melting in the heat of his gaze.

Wildon placed the tray on the table.

"Please sit down, Mother Glenmore, and do join us, Jacques. Shall I get your driver?"

Tia saw her mother glare at Wildon so fiercely, it was a

wonder that he didn't have first degree burns.

"My driver has already eaten."

"Pity. I made more than enough."

"Don't I know you? From the Sierra club?" Jacques questioned Wildon.

Wildon smiled. "Yes! Jacques Fourant--right?"

Jacques nodded. Wildon shook his hand.

"Nice to see you again! You'll have to try my handiwork here. I attempted to make these sandwiches taste like the ones served at that meeting four months ago."

Tia watched Wildon lift up a sandwich to admire it. She knew he must have done a considerable amount of manipulating. Pink shrimp salad sat between thin slices of pumpernickel bread garnished with dill. She did have dill growing in her garden, but the shrimp and pumpernickel did not come from her kitchen. Still, the sandwiches did look tempting.

Wildon ate the small sandwich in two bites, and then closed his eyes. "The dill is the perfect touch." He started heaping plates with his handiwork. Tia shrugged and sat down. She realized how hungry she felt and reached for a sandwich. When she tasted it, a kind of awe settled on her. She realized that if he hadn't seduced her already, his knack for putting together shrimp salad sandwiches would have enticed her to his bed. His sandwiches were as good as his lovemaking--so exquisite that she could not resist another sample.

She lifted her gaze to his and he gave her another of his arresting smiles, turning her insides to mush. He placed a plate of sandwiches into front of Tia's mother.

"No thank you. I'm trying to watch my weight as well as my sodium."

"You look perfect to me," Jacques commented.

Tia saw her mother blush and nearly gasped. Glancing at Wildon, she saw him toying with the teabag tags hanging from the teapot. Naturally the tags labeled the tea as decaf, but she caught something in his manner that caused a trace of doubt to cloud her trust. She had seen him with that same look before back in the Sifra. His manner stiff and his eyes shuttered. She swallowed hard. That was right before he told her she was his bride.

A small chill shot up her spine as she studied him. What was Wildon up to?

She watched him pour the tea and pass the cups around with her nerves tightening into cold knots. For all she knew, he might snap his fingers and make a goldfish appear swimming around in everyone's cup.

Cautiously, she sipped the tea. It did indeed taste like decaf. Her mother sipped some tea and batted her eyelashes at Jacques who ate ten sandwiches and drank three cups of tea while gazing at Tia's mother like a lovesick puppy.

"I guess it won't hurt to try just one little sandwich." Tia's mother reached for one of the tasty morsels on Jacques plate.

Wildon sat down next to Tia and leaned over to speak softly into her ear. "Should I fix that rock?"

Sheer fright raced through her. "Not right now."

He gave her one of his wide, beatific grins with all his perfect, white teeth. "Later?"

"Maybe."

He appeared confused for a moment but then he shrugged and ate some sandwiches.

"You know, if they build that new nuclear plant, Tia and I will be able to see the smokestacks right over there." Wildon pointed off into the distance.

Tia watched as an odd look crossed her mother's face.

"That would mar this lovely view."

Jacques gave a huge sigh. "If that plant is built, not only our lives but the lives of our grandchildren will be endangered."

"Do you have grandchildren, Jacques?" Angela Glenmore's hand slid over to cover Jacques' hand.

"Two," Jacques stated softly while staring into Angela's eyes. "Would you like to see their photographs?"

"Yes, I would."

"How about tonight?"

"At eight perhaps?"

"Dinner?"

"How sweet of you."

Tia could not believe the look on her mother's face as she smiled at the handsome bodyguard.

"I will be opposing the bill currently in the senate before

this view is ruined," promised Angela.

Jacques nodded before he stuffed another little sandwich in his mouth.

Tia knew her mother had been backing the bill until now. She put her hand on her mother's forehead. "Are you feeling all right, Mom?"

Her mother gently removed her hand. "Don't be silly. I feel perfectly fine, dear." Then she glanced at her watch and sighed. "Thanks so much for the tea, but I do have another one of those dreadful campaign stops." She stood up. "Good-bye, Wildon. Take good care of my Tia."

"It will be my pleasure." Wildon smiled.

Tia watched her mother dismiss the policeman and hurry to her limousine. Jacques got into his own car.

Tia glared at Wildon.

"What did you do to my mother? Did you make her fall in love with Jacques? I knew you were up to something!"

"My priceless bride, would I hurt your sweet mother?" He managed to appear affronted.

She knew he had cast a spell. Somehow, some way-- without snapping his fingers or clapping his hands, he had completely changed her mother. Tia could feel the tears pricking at the back of her eyes. She had been a fool. She had trusted him!

Rushing into the house for a tissue, she saw something that made her heart nearly stop. On the counter in the kitchen, a swirling mist issued from a large opened can. The mixture in the can bubbled and hissed.

Setting her mouth grimly, she could feel fury escalating in her blood. Wildon must have concocted it and poisoned her mother with it. She walked to the counter, fully intending to throw the can and its contents out the door. However, she took only one step before Wildon's hands clamped down upon her shoulders.

"Don't touch that. It's highly unstable. I must remove it with caution."

She struggled to get out of his grasp. "You poisoned my mother!"

"No. I did not."

Something shifted inside Tia. It was as if her heart was

shoved out of place by a cold piece of steel.

"You're lying. You tricked me. You don't love me, you only wanted to get close enough so you could poison my mother. You are no better than that carjacker."

She heard him sigh before he dropped his hands from her shoulders. Silently, he walked over to lift up the can with its noxious contents.

"I hate you! Get out of here!" she screamed.

He turned to look at her and she could only stand there and stare into his soft green eyes.

"I love you, Tia. I always will. Forever. Remember me."

Then he vanished. Slowly, Tia crumbled to the floor.

Chapter Eight

Wildon sat atop the rock bluff in the moonlight and stared down upon Tia's little enclave. From his perch, the whole of the Glenmore Farms Plant Nursery appeared to be about the size of his thumbnail. His sister sat next to him with her long, blond hair dangling down above the precipitous cliff.

"You should go and visit with her," Enid suggested.

"She will still hate me. Her mother cannot win the nomination now. Angela Glenmore is so anti-nuclear that some are labeling her a crackpot."

Enid laughed. "Whatever is that?"

"Not good for a politician."

Enid held out a dandelion puff and blew the seeds away. Wildon saw the gentle silver light from the moon dance upon the small seeds. They floated off, twirling in the air with delicate precision in a gentle and pleasurable way.

Wildon could not bear to watch such a simple delight. It made him more morose. He fisted his hand and then opened it. All the soft, wispy seeds turned into drops of water.

Enid sighed. "Ah, brother prince, you need healing. You should see the wise ones for they can take away the sting of a broken heart."

Wildon shook his head. He clung to each and every memory he had of Tia. If he went to the wise ones, they would make him forget--and he wanted to recall all the precious moments he had spent with her.

"You cannot spend all your time up here with your face as much like stone as the granite. You have succeeded in saving the Sifra. There is much merriment and dancing in our beautiful palace while you sit nursing your misery."

Wildon smoothed his hand along the hard edge of the rock. It had gone through great pressure and survived.

"The stones talk of the great upheavals that made them into mountains. I find comfort in the tales."

Enid shook her head. "The stones take a whole day to utter

one word."

Wildon shrugged. He had already told Enid to leave him
alone, but she had not paid any attention to him. She didn't
seem to realize that he wasn't simply grieving over his lost
love, he was also watching out for Tia. Something was going to
happen. Unfortunately, he didn't know exactly what. His mind
was too clouded with sorrow.

"I have composed a ballad about you." Enid picked up the
harp at her side.

"Don't." His voice sounded harsh, like the croak of a frog
in a midnight pond.

"It's quite lively," Enid went on. "No one will be able to
resist joining in the dance when I play it. I will sing of my hero
brother with pride."

"I am not a hero."

"Of course you are!"

"Our father, the king, is not pleased with me."

"You disobeyed him."

Wildon turned to frown at his sister. "How could I make
Tia forget me when I will never forget her?" A stab of grief
knifed through him and he closed his eyes.

He felt Enid's tender touch upon his shoulder.

"In time, your heartache will fade. Our father does not
know what it is like to love a human, but he does love you--that
is what counts."

"She was the one I had chosen. She was my bride." His
voice grew strained.

Enid gave his hand a squeeze. "You really should see her.
Then you would know how she feels."

"I *know* how she feels. She said I was no better than the
carjacker."

"That was said in anger. Humans say terrible things when
they are hurt."

Wildon nodded and opened his eyes. "At any rate, she is
not there. She left yesterday and has not come back. She has a
new car. It is white, like the moon."

He glanced at the moon once more and sighed.

After a few more moments, Enid left him alone. He went
back to staring at the plant nursery while the morning light rose
in the east. He felt tension in the air. He turned his face to the

south and spotted a large tanker truck careening along the country highway in the red dawn. The truck sped along the snaking ribbon of road that curled around the mountains. Wildon stood up and frowned. The vehicle moved too quickly for the tight turns and narrow lanes. His heart began to race. He knew imminent danger when he saw it.

The truck barreled on, heading north in the direction of Tia's property. Wildon ran his hand through his hair. That truck would surely miss a turn and crash. Most tanker trucks carried flammable, highly explosive liquids.

He was watching an environmental disaster about to happen. What should he do?

He picked up the mantle he had laid upon the rock and threw it across his shoulders. Within a moment he stood beside the sign in front of Tia's home. All appeared dark and silent inside. His heart filled with a sad ache, but he knew he did not have time to linger. Swirling his hands, he set up a thick mist to enclose the property in safety.

Then he heard and felt the explosion. The ground beneath his feet shook with such force that he stumbled to his knees. He glanced up and saw a huge noxious plume billow into the sky. He covered his face with the mantle and vanished.

* * * *

Tia padded softly across the carpet and turned on the television in her mother's condominium. She had slept at Mom's place after they had gotten back late from a night out at her mother's favorite restaurant. It had been a very pleasant evening. Tia could hardly believe the change that Wildon had wrought upon her mother.

Her mother was *happy*. The imperious politician who could strong-arm a bill through the Senate had faded into a memory. In her place was the mother Tia remembered from her childhood. The one with a wealth of genuine smiles and light laughter.

Her mother was not going to become a United States president, and she didn't care. Angela Glenmore's blood pressure was well under control and she was now dating Jacques on a regular basis. Tia liked Jacques. He seemed to be a very honorable gentleman. They had talked for hours last night and he seemed so infatuated with her mother that Tia felt tears pricking at the back of her eyes.

Being in love was an awesome experience and she had only known it for such a very short time.

Tia sniffed. It seared her heart to remember the passion she had shared with Wildon. Unfortunately, whether she was awake or asleep it seemed as though she could not escape the burning imprint of ecstasy he had left on her soul.

Turning to the morning news, she mixed up a bowl of oatmeal for herself. She promised herself that she would make a genuine effort to eat some of it. She needed her strength since she had to get back to her nursery and fill an order for a wedding today before the sun rose much higher.

That thought brought on a gloomy chill. She had dreamed of her own magic wedding to Wildon again during the night. It seemed that lately all her dreams involved Wildon. The truth was that she missed him--hungered for him--loved him--even though he had only used her to get close to her mother.

The raw hurt had not left her. Of course, what he had done was criminal. He should not have altered her mother's personality with that horrible potion. It could have been poison. She would have had him prosecuted if he hadn't disappeared.

Yet, the transformation of her mother had been nothing short of a miracle. Her mother had changed for the *better*.

Tia bit her lip to keep it from trembling. She stirred the oatmeal and poured in some milk. The color of her breakfast reminded her of new, button mushrooms and of Wildon stroking her skin. She shivered and sat down.

The television finally caught her attention and Tia gasped when she saw the twisted wreckage of the tanker truck at the bottom of a ravine she knew to be not more than five hundred feet from the edge of her property.

She turned up the sound and peered at the picture on the screen. In the background, she could see the wooden sign, but past that she could see only a heavy white fog hiding her cabin and the greenhouses.

She glanced outside through the condo's windows where it was sunny and clear--but sometimes atmospheric conditions were strange in the mountains.

Frowning, she turned her attention back to the news where they reported that the truck had been carrying sulfuric acid. So far, one was seriously injured, but about 20 people were treated at hospitals for burning throats and skin exposure to the chemical. The surrounding area had been evacuated.

Tia stood up. Would she be able to fill that wedding order? Could she get into the nursery? She watched as the paramedics loaded a man onto a stretcher. When the camera panned in closer, Tia saw that it was Wildon lying there! He had a deep bloody gash on his cheek!

Sudden panic swept through her, chilling her to the core. She forgot about her oatmeal. Her heart pounded as she dashed for her shoes and her jacket, but she couldn't find her keys. She raced around retracing her steps, trying to remember what she had done with her car keys when she had entered the condo so late last night.

Her mother came out of the bedroom as Tia was yanking all the cushions off the couch.

"Whatever is the matter, dear?"

"Wildon! I saw him on TV! He's hurt! And I can't find my keys!" She let out a sob and sank down on one of the cushions.

Her mother glanced at the TV and then lifted something off the counter. "Aren't these yours?"

Tia lunged for the keys. "Thanks." Attempting to catch her breath, tie her shoelaces, and dash away a tear at the same time, she asked, "Which hospital do you think the paramedics would use?"

Her mother reached for a phone book. "I know I probably caused your breakup. I-I'm sorry."

Tia stilled. Her mother had no idea about the truth--and she couldn't tell her. Floundering, she mumbled, "He wasn't in love with me."

"Nonsense." Her mother put on her reading glasses and flipped through the phone book listings. "You had a fight because I was misled by that foolish detective."

Tia sagged against the counter. "We did have a fight, but it was about something else. I thought Wildon was wrong, but maybe he could have been doing the right thing--it's just the way he went about it."

Her mother nodded as if she understood. Picking up the

phone, she started punching in numbers. "You just sit here and finish your oatmeal, young lady. I'll find where our poor Wildon is in a jiffy."

Feeling wretched, Tia plopped down on the chair next to her oatmeal and stared at it. Regrets tormented her. She heard his last words to her over and over again.

I love you, Tia. I always will. Forever.

Meanwhile, her mother scribbled something down on a piece of paper.

"Okay, dear. I've found him. Let me step into a pair of jeans and we'll go see him."

Tia jumped up. "Mom! You take too long! You have to put your makeup on and your suit and--"

"I'm not posing for the cameras anymore, dear."

"I'll drive myself! You drive too slowly."

"I'm driving."

Tia heard the steel in her mother's voice and realized that some things about her mother hadn't changed at all.

"You are trembling, sweetheart. You calm yourself down and pray. We'll get there in good time and in one piece."

Chapter Nine

"How do you do?" Wildon gave the nurse his most ingratiating smile. "I really feel great."

"Good. We'll take care of that cut very soon." The nurse pumped up the blood pressure cuff.

Wildon drummed his fingers on the bed's metal railing. The last place he needed to be was in a human hospital. Right now, the sulfuric acid was being diluted by careless humans who didn't consider what the runoff would do to the streams. He put his hand on his forehead. "The frogs, fish, and turtles--they're all going to die."

The nurse gave him a stern look. "You must hold still while I'm taking your blood pressure." She took the cuff off and promptly proceeded to wrap it around his other arm.

Wildon clenched his teeth together and decided that putting a wart on her nose would not help matters.

"Wouldn't you like to have one less patient?"

She put the ends of the stethoscope in her ears. "The doctor will look at you in just a few minutes." She started pumping up the blood pressure cuff once more.

Wildon winced. He had been through this procedure before and discovered that the Sidhe had very low blood pressure, but he couldn't remember what was normal for a human.

"What's a good blood pressure reading?"

"You are not supposed to talk either." Her sharp tone brooked no argument.

Wildon turned his head to stare at the line of mercury dropping down on the gauge. He decided that halfway down should be good--humans always averaged things out. He moved his index finger. The mercury line halted.

The nurse glared at the gauge. "Something must be wrong with this machine."

"What does it say?" Wildon asked, trying his best to look innocent.

"Well, it's okay, but it isn't supposed to stop so quickly."

"Oh." Wildon moved his index finger once more and the line moved slowly downward.

"Hmm. It seems to be all right now."

"Thank you. I'll go home now."

"No, you won't. The doctor has to stitch up that nasty cut. He won't be long."

The nurse pulled the curtain open, rolled out the blood pressure machine, closed the curtain, and went to check out the next victim.

Wildon reached up to feel the cut on his cheek. It was already an inch shorter than it had been an hour before. He slid off the gurney. He would not allow a doctor to use a needle and thread on him. He peered out at the scene in the emergency room from the edge of the curtain. Everything seemed to be in a total state of chaos--which was good for him. He could make a clean getaway. He ducked underneath the gurney and found his backpack. Unzipping it, he reached in and pulled out his old green mantle.

"Excuse me, Mr. Forest. I'd like to ask you a few questions. I'm told you rescued the trucker."

The curtain opened. Wildon flinched and turned to see a policeman. Swallowing hard, he stuffed the mantle back inside the backpack.

"The trucker reeked of wine and swung at me when I took him out of the truck cab. It was not a pleasant experience."

"I can understand that, sir. However, it was fortunate that you just happened to be right there when the truck went off the road."

Wildon tensed. He didn't trust cops--they asked tricky questions deliberately. He nodded.

The policeman continued, "The trucker has some severe burns, yet you seem to have escaped with nothing more than the cut on your cheek."

"I got there *after* the explosion."

"How long was that?"

Sounds from outside the curtain rushed in at Wildon. The doctor was getting closer. He clenched his hands as the anxiety built up. He had to escape!

"I don't know. The force of the blast knocked me down."

"Did you black out?"

Wildon felt his control slipping. "No!"

"I realize that this has been an upsetting incident for you, sir. However--"

Wildon waved his hand and the policeman stopped with his mouth partially open. Wildon smiled. The cop would be in suspended animation for about five minutes, which was all Wildon needed.

He pulled out his mantle again, draped it around his shoulders and began to fasten it. Reaching once more for the backpack on the gurney, he turned and saw his beloved Tia staring at him from the edge of the curtain. Fear and longing collided inside him at the same time. The backpack fell out of his hands.

"Are you okay?"

He heard the tremor in her voice. He locked his gaze with hers, becoming trapped in those stunning sapphire pools glistening with unshed tears.

"Has the cat got your tongue?" Angela Glenmore came up behind Tia.

"C-cat? T-tongue?" Wildon stammered.

"That's another idiom. It means...." Tia sobbed. "Oh, Wildon! I've missed you." She flew into in his arms in less than a heartbeat.

Wildon closed his eyes and savored the feel of her. The warmth, the scent, the touch of her skin against his erased the dull ache of suffering that had haunted him.

"Has the cat got your tongue?" he muttered into her ear.

"What?" Tia sniffed.

"I've missed you, too." He touched her fiery hair. Finer than corn silk, it set his pulse throbbing.

"--we do need your help in...."

Wildon glanced at policeman. The befuddled cop blinked and scratched his head. Then he saw Tia's mother and snapped to attention. "Senator Glenmore, how nice to see you again."

"Officer Blake. Such a pleasure." Angela Glenmore shook the cop's hand.

That's when the doctor stepped into the small curtained alcove. "What have we here?"

Wildon felt the blood pool in his feet. "Nothing, doctor. Just a scratch. It doesn't need stitches."

"It could use a few." Tia's hand touched his cheek.

"No! It doesn't hurt at all!"

"Wildon? Are you afraid of the doctor?" Tia's gentle smile teased him.

"Perhaps, he would like to see his own doctor," Angela suggested.

"Yes--I would! Thank you, Mother Glenmore! That's exactly what I will do." He noticed the change in her--all for the better, of course. However, that positive change had been none of his doing. Though he knew Tia did not believe that. Could she ever welcome him back into her heart once more? He had to find out.

"I'd like to go home first." He heard the unmistakable sound of the strain in his own voice. He felt so uncertain. It was a novel emotion for him--the prince, the son of the king. Everything had changed because of Tia. Everything that mattered.

"Home?" Tia's voice quivered.

He saw the spark of fear in her eyes and felt the ache as his throat tightened.

"To *our* home, my dearest wife."

He could not mistake the hope he caught spreading across her face. However, it quickly faded.

"But they've evacuated people from that area. I don't know what shape the nursery will be in when I return--I don't know when I'll be able to get back. All my plants m-may be dead."

Wildon watched her twist her hands. He reached out and took them in his. Her hands were cold and trembled.

"Your plant nursery is safe."

Her brow furrowed.

"There is a most unusual mist around your property--a very thick fog." He smiled at her. "It will protect everything from the acid."

"Can I give you a lift?" Angela offered.

Wildon scooped Tia up in his arms. "No thank you, Mother. I can lift Tia myself."

He headed toward the elevator. He heard Tia sigh.

"Mom's been really nice--a lot like she used to be before she became a hard-nosed politician."

"Her nose doesn't appear to be any harder than anyone else's nose."

"That's just another expression. She was so assertive ... so forceful ... so much like a Sherman tank."

"Would you please push that button for me?" Wildon asked as they reached the elevator. He had learned that it was far, far better to push the button than to yank the elevator down the shaft.

Tia's dainty finger pressed the button. "Mom's a lot more relaxed. Her blood pressure is normal--she and Jacques are so good for each other...." Her voice faltered. "What I'm trying to say is that I guess your concoction was good for her. I'm sorry--but I didn't understand."

He whispered as he gazed into her eyes. "I never gave your mother the potion. Jacques' love is what transformed her."

"B-but she's a completely different person."

"I'm a different Sidhe because of you."

"Me?"

He nodded. The wonder of Tia's smile lit up his heart.

Her hands slid around his neck and he drew her closer. He could feel the momentum building, the lurch in his heart, the fire in his loins.

The elevator doors opened and he stepped inside.

"What floor?" Tia's hand hovered near the buttons.

"Just close the door." Wildon said. "We'll be home in a moment."

"You won't stay with me forever. You won't want to lose your magic."

Her words sounded hollow and he felt a pang in his heart. The heat of her body radiated all through him. How many days had he suffered without her? The pain had been almost unbearable.

"Your love is all the magic I need."

He watched as she closed her eyes and turned her face away from him. A chill wound its way through him as if the sun had gone dark.

"You're just saying that. You'll walk right out of my life if you can't snap your fingers and make ice or make spoons dance ... or make your mist."

"Forever can be a long time without someone to love." He had said the same words to her once in the Sifra, but now he realized the full weight of that expression.

"You'll get old and die."

"I will die without your love." He could not prevent the huskiness in his voice for he knew it was true. He would fade away into a shadow if he sat much longer on the mountain.

Her sapphire gaze flashed upon him once more and he felt his soul grow warm.

"What about your family ... your sister and your father, the king?"

"They can come and visit us."

"Will you really stay with me?"

He saw the earnest hope shining in her face.

"As long as we both shall live."

He drew her closer and their lips met even as the mantle transported them home.

The End

EPPIE award-winning author, Penelope Marzec grew up along the Jersey shore. She started reading romances at a young age even though her mother told her they would ruin her mind, which they did and she became hopelessly hooked on happy endings. A member of the New Jersey Romance Writers, the Liberty States Writers Fiction Writers and EPIC, Penelope writes for three publishers in two subgenres of romance--inspirational and paranormal.

Visit her website at **www.penelopemarzec.com** to learn more about her latest releases, appearance, and contests.

Check out her musings at her blog:
http://penelopemarzec.blogspot.com

Follow her on Twitter and Facebook, too.